True Tales of The Supernatural: Real Christmas Ghost Stories

Volume Five

Tina Vantyler

Published by Zanderam London Press
First printing 2023
Paperback ISBN: 978-1-7399072-8-0
Copyright © 2023, Tina Vantyler
Website: **tinavantylerbooks.com**

CONTENTS

INTRODUCTION

THE 12 GHOSTS OF CHRISTMAS

GREETINGS OF THE SEASON, fellow fear enthusiasts. May I present my fifth collection of genuine ghost stories, a treasury that is truly special as each tale unfolds against the enchantingly eerie backdrop of the Christmas season.

Gathering to tell stories is as old as humanity itself, and our fondness for supernatural fables during the festive season originates from Winter Solstice customs dating back many centuries.

According to ancient folklore, December's Winter

Solstice, the longest night of the year, and the subsequent 12 Days of Christmas, beginning on Christmas Day, are believed to signify a period when the barrier between the living and the dead becomes blurred, allowing spirits the freedom to wander our world. These traditions intertwine with beliefs in divination and omens, where occurrences during these 12 days – whether in dreams, the behaviour of animals, or weather patterns – may be regarded as predictions for the coming year.

Thus the number 12 holds mystical significance during this festive period, and what better way to honour it than with the same number of ghostly accounts?

Christmas arrives cloaked in winter's icy embrace and shrouded in prolonged darkness. In our minds at least, it's a time when a fire crackles in the hearth, rain pelts the windowpanes and chill winds howl outside, setting the stage for supernatural stories and spectral encounters.

As you embark on this journey through a dozen haunting tales, may you find comfort in the warmth of your surroundings and the company of loved ones, even as you shudder with anticipation at the harrowing accounts to come.

Brace yourself for offerings such as:

~ The eerie hotel resident who liked to watch in *Rapunzel...*

~ The terrible act of kindness in *One Last Holiday...*

~ The man with death in his eyes in *Deadbeat Daniel...*

~ The wraith who craved togetherness in *Misery Loves Company...*

~ The unnatural echoes that tormented a family in *Upstairs, Downstairs...*

~ The unholy horror in the library in *By The Book...*

And remember, amidst the sparkle of tinsel and the joy of gift-giving, the spirit of Christmas isn't always merry. Sometimes, it lurks in the shadows, eager to trace icy fingers down your spine...

ONE

BY THE BOOK

Joel's find when his parents moved house brought back memories that were most unwelcome...

My GHOST STORY BEGINS in the present, although the real tale happened nearly three decades ago.

In December 2022, Mum and Dad were downsizing from our family home because me and my two sisters had long since flown the nest.

'That means you all have to take any stuff you've left here,' said my mum on the phone. 'We've sorted it as best we can. Your old toys are long gone, but there's still your schoolbooks, medals, birthday cards plus odds and ends. It's in bags, already packed.'

I think most people find it poignant to say goodbye to their childhood home. After chucking the bags on the back seat of my car, I took a mooch around the rooms, remembering kids' parties, the kitchen table where I did my homework and we had countless family meals, and the bedroom which, as the only boy, had been mine for years, to the fury of my sisters, who were forced to share. Aggie and Petra were six and seven years older than me.

'We're moving to the new place on Friday,' said Dad as they saw me to my car. 'Just in time for Christmas.'

'Yes, come for lunch on Christmas Day,' said my mum. 'It'll be just the three of us as the girls are away.'

My mother's cooking was notoriously awful, and I didn't fancy one of her dried-out roasts. But given that my girlfriend, Isla, had ditched me and moved out of our flat last weekend, I'd probably go for something to do.

At home, I tipped the first bag onto the floor. Mum was quite a hoarder and I didn't need every exercise book from my first day of primary school all the way up to fifth year. Placing those in the 'chuck' pile, I struggled to find something to keep. Then I saw my old diary, with its glossy black plastic cover and little gold lock that never worked, and laughed.

I'd forgotten all about this! Unhooking the clasp, I recalled Miss Timms, my new teacher when I was eight. A few weeks into the September term, she'd urged me to start a diary. 'Your creative writing could be so much better if you practised at home,' she'd told me. 'A diary will help. Write down things you notice and don't censor yourself. It's private, just for you, but you'll get insights that can go in your essays. Life experiences.'

I'd got this one the previous Christmas but not bothered with it much.

I made a coffee, took a seat on the sofa and, heels on the footstool, prepared to take a journey back to the world of eight-year-old Joel.

Now I wish I'd thrown that diary away without opening it.

The size of a Christmas card, but with a thick spine, it was a page a day. After filling in my name and address in the front, along with the names of my parents, sisters, and our two cats, from January onwards the occasional page was filled with the cramped, near-illegible scrawl I got told off for daily at school.

Pausing here and there to chuckle at a memory, I flicked past school trips, visits to relatives, rude comments my friends had made and the like.

Then, in November, the nature of the entries changed dramatically.

Saturday 5 November

"Mummy has agreed with Miss Timms that she'll take me to the local library every two weeks so I can choose a book. That's OK, although I won't read them. I can skip through them and pretend I have.

"Today me and Mum came for the first time, even though it's Bonfire Night. While she was in the grown-up bit, I stayed in the children's part. It's very big and I don't think I can manage to read all those books. I like the thin ones best.

The fat ones have too many words and not enough pictures.

"I was the only child here, but I saw a man looking at me from behind the shelves, peeping around a corner. I didn't like him.

"I grabbed the nearest book and ran to find Mum."

I put the diary down and sat back. The library was still there, although I hadn't been in it for years. A grey building with arches that reminded me of a church, it had smelt of floor polish and cabbage. I couldn't remember a man, although reading this made me uncomfortable. After a few sips of coffee, I carried on.

The following days were full of the usual school and family stuff. Then, 10 days on:

Saturday 19 November

"Me and Mum came to change my library book. I'd forgotten about the man. But he was here, closer this time. He's dressed all in black, in like a dress, and has a tiny head and a face like a rat. He walked over and I think he wanted to talk to me. But he has no feet so I'm not sure how he walks. More floating or hovering, like a big black bird but upright and close to the ground. Not like a real person moves. I grabbed another book and got away before he could reach me. He almost touched me, and my legs went all shaky. I think he's dead."

I twisted in my seat. *He's dressed all in black, in like a dress, and has a tiny head and a face like a rat.* A dim memory was surfacing. Nightmares I'd had at the time. My sisters telling me not to be a cry-baby when I'd run into their room after one of my bad dreams.

I think he's dead. What?

The next entries were lists. School work I had to do. Buses I'd seen – I was a bus-spotter then. Toys I wanted for Christmas.

Until December.

Saturday 3 December

"I told Mummy I don't want to visit the library anymore, but she made me go. 'Miss Timms says the books are doing you good, improving your stories,' she said. 'And I've got through my novels. You're coming.'

"'But there's a man in the children's bit and he's not right,' I said. 'He shouldn't be there.'

"'Don't fuss, Joel,' she said. 'That will be the librarian. There to help you.'

"She pushed me away when I followed her to the adult area. 'Shoo!' she said. 'Pop your old book on the counter and get another.'

"'Come with me?' I pleaded.

"'Your sisters are right about you,' she said. 'Attention-seeking. Go get your new book, check it out, then meet me in the foyer.'

"I knew he'd be there. A girl my age sat on a stool, but he ignored her and stood staring at me. I moved to look at the books but kept him in sight so he couldn't get near me. When the girl's mum called her over and she left – and got a hug, which I never did! – he floated right up to me, bent low and put his face close to mine. Before I could see him properly, I squeezed my eyes shut and ran off, tripping over a stool.

"I didn't care what my mummy thought, what the fat librarian lady thought, or what my sisters would say if Mum told them. Crying, I ran in to the adult bit and found her with a pile of paperbacks.

'The man is here, he's dead, and he's after me!' I sobbed.

"She shook my hand off, embarrassed by the stares of the other grown-ups, and dragged me out of the building.

"At home, Mum took my Gameboy and two of my favourite Ninja Turtles off me.

'You'll get these back tomorrow,' she said, 'if you're good and stop talking rubbish about dead men in the library.' My mum wasn't a very kind person, and Dad was usually at work and didn't defend us from her even when he was home."

The next three days were blank. Then:

Wednesday 7 December

"I wrote a scary story about the man for Miss Timms. She said it was 'imaginative' and read it out to the class. I was proud, yet scared because I'd told a person outside my family about him.

"At lunchtime, I followed Miss Timms to the staff room and told her I hadn't made the story about the man up.

"'He's real,' I said, 'And those things happened.'

"Miss Timms was cross. 'A strong imagination is one thing,' she said, 'and will help you go far. On the other hand, a liar doesn't prosper.'

"'What's prosper?' I asked.

"'It means you'll live a life of misery and failure if you tell lies,' she said. Then she went into the staff room and slammed the door shut so hard it wobbled.

"I had a cry in the boys' toilets and went to find my friends."

I felt sad for young Joel, and I connected with him, told by the people he trusted to keep his important thoughts and feelings to himself. That had been part of the problem with Isla.

That entry was followed by more blank pages. No wonder I'd lost enthusiasm for my diary. Then, as I continued through the book, I realised with a jolt that I knew what was coming.

Because I remembered.

Could I bear to read it?

I had to.

Sunday 18 December

"He was in my room last night. I knew he'd come because he knows I'm all alone. "The day before, I'd asked Dad if I could share a room with Aggie, the least horrible sister. Dad wouldn't have it. 'Neither of them wants to share with you,' he said. 'You're lucky. Enjoy your space and stop moaning.'

"At bedtime, I kept the light on as long as I could. Mummy came to switch it off at 10 o'clock. 'This is late enough for a boy of eight,' she said, closing my door.

I hadn't been to the library for two weeks and it was Saturday, the day me and Mum normally went. She'd been to see a friend in hospital, so we didn't have to go and I'd been very relieved. But in bed, I'd had a bad feeling.

"I'd dragged the curtains back as far as they'd go to let in the moonlight and I kept my eyes open as long as I could. I must have dropped off, though, because I suddenly woke up.

"There he was, standing at the bottom of my bed in front of the window. Around his neck was a white band, like the collar you see on dogs, gleaming in the moonlight. The man didn't move. Then he smiled, and it was the most horrible thing I have ever EVER seen. Podgy lips curling almost to his ears, jagged, yellow stumpy teeth, big nostrils, the nose bent to one side like he'd been punched. And black eyes, damp and shiny.

"Breathing hard, I pulled the covers over my head. Maybe I fainted because next time I looked, it was still nighttime, but I was on my own.

"My family don't care about me. Miss Timms doesn't care. I'm leaving home today. I don't know where I'll go.

"I just can't see that man again."

My chest felt tight with anguish for this small boy who felt so abandoned and tormented. Talking to you brings it all back. The feelings I'd locked away for 28 years.

I flipped to the end of the diary. The last few pages were empty.

It didn't matter because I was aware of what happened next.

I did run away that Sunday. I packed my school rucksack with a bottle of water and my favourite toys, sneaked onto a bus and hid at the back. After an hour, I ended up in a country park but, not sure where to go, I began to feel scared and confused. And so cold, the sharp air biting at the flesh of my face and hands, making my nose tingle.

Meanwhile, my parents freaked out and called the police, who found me after a tip-off when I stole a sandwich from the park cafe.

Mum scooped me up in a big hug, the first she'd given me since I was tiny, when the police brought me home. Dad gave me crisps and even my sisters talked to me, wanting to know about my adventure.

Apart from giving me a major telling-off, my

parents didn't ask much about why I'd left, although I recall I tried to tell them again about the man. But there must have been a family conference, because from then on I shared a bedroom with Aggie, while Petra got mine.

Christmas came a week or so after my escape to the country, but I remained silent and sullen throughout the gift-giving and usual festivities. No one noticed.

I never saw the man again. And Miss Timms continued to be cool towards me, so I was relieved to move to a new class the following year.

But there are two postscripts to this story.

❧❧❧❧❧ ❦❦❦❦❦

Putting the diary down, I searched online for the library. Astonishingly, it had been built in the nineteenth century as a school by a vicar. There had been a scandal, the nature of which wasn't clear, but he'd died in his thirties before the school became established, possibly taking his own life. The building fell into disrepair before being renovated as a library in the 1980s.

I couldn't find a photo of the vicar, which even at a

distance of 20-plus years was a relief. My subconscious mind had blocked out the image of the terrible face I described in my diary, so I couldn't conjure it up in my mind's eye.

This vicar, who would have worn a white dog collar, was the correct age for the man who had hung around me in the library and at home with such malevolence. Seeing a picture of him would, I feared, cause that face to plague my dreams for the rest of my life.

The second postscript is even sadder in a way. I went to my parents' for Christmas lunch as arranged, watching as if from a distance as Mum bustled around the kitchen, basting the turkey, peeling sprouts, stirring her homemade cranberry sauce and asking me superficial if well-meaning questions about my life while my dad, as usual, sat silently in a chair, bent over a crossword and making no effort to assist unless begged.

Having revisited my childhood via my diary, I understand more of why I don't feel anything other than a perfunctory emotional connection to them both.

That period all those years ago when I was a small,

frightened boy, desperately in need of their love and support while they did nothing to help me, has ruined our relationship for good.

TWO

UPSTAIRS, DOWNSTAIRS

***Keely was delighted that her dad could offer
her family a home for Christmas.
But what were those noises...?***

THE PROBLEMS BEGAN AS soon as we moved into the
house.

Our baby, Tara, was six months old when me and
my partner John took the place in November. Her
birth had been long and difficult, and I often felt tired.
A haunting was the last thing I needed – not that
there's ever a good time for one.

My dad, a property developer and builder, had given us the two-up, two-down terraced house rent-free for a couple of years. 'It's not quite finished,' he'd told me. 'Still a few bits to do before it's ready for paying tenants. But you three are welcome to it for now.'

Dad knew me and John had money problems and I felt lucky that he could help us out. It was so expensive to rent these days, let alone buy, and all my friends were struggling to find decent accommodation.

'This will do while you get on your feet,' Dad told me, unlocking the door as his removal men unloaded the few items we'd brought from our old flat. 'You've got a front and back room, a bathroom and two good-sized bedrooms. There's a new cot for Tara in the front bedroom.'

'Thanks, Dad,' I said, kissing his bristly cheek. 'It means a lot to us to have our own place in time for our first family Christmas.'

Me and John had met in our teens and had hoped to get married and start a family in the future. But it seems Tara had other ideas so, when I found myself pregnant at 20, we decided to go with the flow. And here we were, a ready-made family of three by our 22nd birthdays.

This was the first time we'd seen the house and, as I carried a kicking Tara in, Dad gave us the grand tour. The front door led straight into a small front room with a two-seater sofa and cream walls.

'The front and back rooms had hardboard covering the original Edwardian fireplaces,' he said, stroking the tiled top of this one. 'We ripped it off, so you have one in each room. They've been swept, so you can use them if you like.

'Small landing,' he said, pausing before passing through to the next room. 'The bedrooms lead straight off the stairs.'

'Small?' said John to me. 'It's, like, two feet square! And look at those stairs. Death trap.'

I had to admit the stairs were very narrow, and steep, too. 'I'm glad I'm not still pregnant,' I said. 'I'd probably have overbalanced and toppled down.' The space was dark, not helped by the chocolate carpet Dad had fitted.

Dad continued his tour. 'Back room, your fireplace, another sofa, a comfy chair and a folding dining table.'

Opposite the exit from the hall was the kitchen door.

'It's certainly *compact*,' said John, an edge to his voice as he walked through the narrow kitchen to another door. 'Bathroom downstairs? I'm not used to them being on the ground floor.'

'These houses were built without bathrooms,' said Dad patiently. 'We knocked down the outdoor loo and put in an extension.'

'A very small extension,' said John under his breath. He didn't earn much in his job as a warehouse packer. And I knew he felt embarrassed that he couldn't afford to support us. John was competitive with my dad, full of resentment that Dad could provide what he couldn't and that we were obliged to accept my father's charity.

Dad's face told me he was struggling not to be curt with John when Tara let out a wail. Babies were always a good distraction.

'Tara needs feeding,' I declared, plopping into the easy chair behind me and unbuttoning my shirt. As Tara latched on, I spotted another door opposite with a latch, rather than a knob like the others. 'What's that door, Dad? A cupboard? We could do with more storage in here.'

Dad crossed the floor to the doorway and flicked a light switch. 'No, that's the cellar,' he said, opening the door and pushing it back against the wall. Even with the contentment and security of Tara at my breast as I cradled her head, I couldn't stop the shudder that went through me.

'When I said the place wasn't finished,' said Dad, 'this is the area we hadn't got round to. It'll be a hell of a job to make it into a basement room, with the waterproofing and whatnot, so it can wait.'

A dank, damp smell wafted up from below the stairs. Above Dad's head hung a single bulb, barely illuminating the dark space, and I could just about see a square landing, like the one in the hall.

John stalked over, looking past my dad. 'Those steps look dangerous. Are they glistening with wet? Bloody Nora, if the stairs to the bedrooms are a death trap, Tara's got no chance if she falls down these.' He turned to me. 'I don't think this is the right house for us, Keely. I don't want you and Tara breathing in damp, either.'

Although I didn't fancy the thought of the creepy

cellar either, I knew this was John trying to put my dad's generosity down again, so I leaped to his defence. 'This place is perfect,' I said firmly. 'We'll be happy here and we're going to have a lovely first Christmas. In a couple of years, we'll have saved up and can move into our own house. I can go back to work part-time soon.'

Dad shrugged. 'There's a bit of rubbish down there from the last owners. Don't worry though, no pentagrams on the wall or haunted dolls' houses.' He chuckled. 'Just a few old bits of furniture and crates of stuff, like bottles.

'The neighbours on either side are friendly. A young couple with a kid or two to the right, and an old lady to the left. She's been here for decades.'

'We'll keep this door shut,' said John, leaning past my dad rudely and pulling it to. 'I'll put a proper lock on it.'

John went to make tea while me and Dad talked about what else we needed. Tara finished nursing and was asleep by the time my boyfriend brought our drinks through. 'I'll tuck her up on the sofa under her blanket,' I said. 'Watch her, Dad, while me and John check out the bedrooms.'

The same size as the rooms beneath them, both fireplaces had been taken out and the spaces plastered over. We were to have the rear bedroom, its window overlooking the back door to the left and the tiled path to the tiny garden.

Forget-me-not blue walls with patterned curtains and a big bed, Tara's new cot to the left, nearest the door. I raised my eyebrows at John. 'Yeah, it will do,' he said, hugging me. We clattered down the stairs, the walls indeed so narrow I could slide my hands down either side as I went, which I welcomed even though there was a banister, given that they were so steep.

Tara slept peacefully on the sofa. Dad, on the other hand, holding his tea, had a look of alarm on his face, which he changed into a smile as we came in.

'I'll leave you kids to it,' he said, rising. 'Grant's outside. We're off to view another property.' Grant was his business partner.

I tucked Tara's blanket around her, then John and I took turns to stow stuff in the various rooms. We'd heard the local fish and chip shop was good, so, after a cod and chips dinner, I had an early night with Tara.

John had pulled the bed away from the corner so we both had space to get in and out. I'd sleep by Tara's cot, while John would be on the window side. She wasn't sleeping through the night at this stage, which meant we weren't either.

That first night she was particularly unsettled, waking us with her mewling every hour. 'I'll take her, babe,' said John, after I'd brought her into bed and that hadn't helped.

Off they went downstairs, and I fell asleep again. I woke at 6.30am to find Tara awake in her cot, burbling to herself. No John.

'Let's find your dad, my girl,' I said, lifting her out and carefully making my way down the treacherous stairs.

The house was toasty warm already and there in the lounge was John, breakfast TV on as he knelt by the fireplace polishing something.

'I had a look in that cellar,' he said. 'It stinks of soil and damp and there's only the one bulb at the top of the stairs, so you can't see much. There's a tiny window, but it's so dirty it doesn't let much light in. And there's plenty of junk. But look, I found these.

They're brass.'

He showed me a shovel, brush, tongs and poker with a stand and a coal bucket, a round design beaten into the side.

Seeing my grumpy partner – so undomesticated that he wouldn't wash up unless I threatened to hide the TV remote on football match days – cleaning like this made me uncomfortable.

'I'll rub them down with this cloth and get some brass polish later. They're tarnished, but they'll do nicely.' He waved the brush at me. 'Let's get a fire guard. Even if we don't make a fire up, they'll look good here. Homely.'

Still holding Tara, who giggled, I was at a loss for words. 'Hon, we can't light fires,' I managed. 'Tara's already sitting on her own. She'll be crawling soon, so we have to hide things that could be dangerous.'

At this point in my story, I bet you're thinking, 'Oh, those objects from the cellar are haunted and they'll cause the trouble.' But that's not what happened.

I was in the kitchen frying bacon while John sat on the floor with Tara when a rumbling sound began. Barely noticeable at first, the noise made a sudden jump in volume as I came in with our bacon sandwiches.

'Is that traffic outside?' said John. The noise continued. 'No, it's in the cellar. But how?' We looked at each other as the volume ramped up. 'I'll check,' he said, jumping to his feet. As he did so, the clattering reached fever pitch, sounding like large pieces of furniture toppling one by one. My John is brave – he used to be a bouncer at a rough club – but he hesitated before putting on the cellar light. The second he pulled open the door, the noises ceased. I watched as he disappeared down the steps, his footsteps cautious. Tara began to howl.

A rattling came from the cellar, followed by a crash. 'John?' I called, comforting Tara.

No answer.

'John!' I cried. Tara struggled in my arms, her face red as I stroked her hair. 'Shush, honey,' I said, the sound of her yelling setting my teeth on edge as I was already tense, the musty smell from the open door settling in my nostrils. 'Shush.'

Another pause.

Then a groan.

Steps slowly ascending the stairs.

John's face appeared, creased by a grimace of pain as he limped in.

'Nothing new in the cellar,' he said, sitting down and rubbing his knees and calves. 'Nothing had fallen over. But... one of the big, heavy crates had been dragged to the bottom of the stairs just around the corner out of sight. I fell over it.'

'Who could have moved the crate,' I cried, 'and made those awful noises?'

'I don't know,' he said. 'But I tell you what. I'm not going down there again until I've dug out my big torch. And your dad needs to put a light in the centre of the cellar. You can't see most of it because of the wall to the left of the stairs. Half the room's in darkness.'

'I have a better idea,' I said. 'Let's not go down there at all.'

'What, and ignore the sounds of God knows what banging around?'

'Yes.'

'No chance. I'm getting my torch for a proper look.'

'Do as you please,' I said huffily. 'I'm going for a

walk to the shops with Tara.'

Bundling us both up against the cold, we found the shop 10 minutes' walk away, as Dad had described. On my way out with my shopping, an elderly woman stopped me on the doorstep. 'Aren't you the girl who's just moved into number 24 up the road?' she asked.

The lady turned out to be our neighbour. We talked and she seemed pleasant, so I promised to invite her over.

Back home, John had forgotten about locating his torch and had assembled our plastic Christmas tree in the corner of the lounge opposite the cellar door.

'What are you doing?' I asked. 'We agreed to put that in the front room and spend less time in here near–' I nodded at the cellar.

'I'm not giving into that,' he said, hanging chocolate ornaments on the branches, 'and this space is perfect for the tree. Help me decorate it with Tara.'

It looked pretty when we'd finished and I went to the bathroom to wash my hands, leaving the door to the kitchen open. The bathroom mirror was opposite the door.

As I focused on the water warming my hands, my

eyes caught movement in the mirror. There behind me in the doorway to the kitchen stood a man.

At first, I thought it was John, but the man, a head taller than me, wore a flat leather cap and was older than my boyfriend. John was short and stocky, whereas this man was tall and thin. His pale, sharp-chinned face was mottled with patches of black, with bare areas around his light blue eyes. And he was staring at me in the mirror.

Too shocked to make a sound, I turned, the soap slipping from my fingers to the floor.

I was alone.

I ran to the lounge. 'Was there someone here?' I exclaimed. John and Tara looked up at me, flustered in the doorway. His surprised expression said it all. While he hadn't seen the man, my distress made him take my words seriously.

A couple of days passed without incident, but me and John were both jumpy and Tara was even harder to settle than in our previous flat, often crying long into the night.

We didn't discuss the problems any further. Even though the cellar alarmed us, when we were both home, we still felt drawn to the lounge and spent most of our time there.

John only had work in the mornings until January, when he went back to full days, so money was very tight. And despite the frosty weather, while John was at the factory, I stayed out of the house as long as I could with Tara, exploring our new neighbourhood.

I sensed the man in the house, especially the kitchen, although I didn't see him. The falling furniture racket happened again, though. Despite the blustery winter weather outside, I took Tara and ran into the garden until it was over.

How a kitchen can be angry I don't know. But that's how ours felt, from the posh spotlights in the ceiling to the dove grey tiled floor. Whenever I had to go in, I'd finish up as fast as possible.

We'd been in the house four weeks and things had been quiet of late. I still hadn't met the young family next door, but I'd seen the old lady, Edith, a couple of times. She was due to visit this afternoon and I welcomed her company. Christmas Day was a week away, and John's parents would be down from Sheffield any day.

I wanted to feel more festive, so I dressed Tara in an elves and reindeer onesie, while I put on my snowman Christmas jumper.

Edith was punctual, arriving at 12.30pm. 'Homemade mince pies,' she said, handing me a box. Holding Tara, Edith stood by the tree looking out of the window as I made tea for us in double-quick time.

Her house was a mirror image of ours and a chest-high wall separated our gardens. Our kitchen windows and back doors faced each other.

'I hope you, John and Tara will be happy here,' she said as I found some old-fashioned carols on the radio for us. 'This hasn't been a cheerful house.'

What a thing to say, I thought. While I didn't want to be rude to our guest, I needed details. 'Not cheerful? How?'

But she didn't reply, instead telling me about her daughter and grandkids, who she was going to stay with for New Year. I let her prattle on, waiting for the right time to jump in and ask for clarification of her initial statement.

Then, as we sat, the noise began in the cellar, the furniture toppling piece by piece, starting low and building up. This time, a metallic grating sound preceded it and I felt the hairs on the back of my neck rise. Edith and I were speechless. Then she spoke.

'You know, I haven't heard that noise for 50 years. But it's not right that we should hear it.'

'It's happened twice before,' I said. 'And when John goes down to check, nothing's been moved, apart from once. And... I saw a man here. In the kitchen. With a very dirty face and wearing a cap.'

I hadn't meant to tell Edith this. She stared at me. 'That makes sense. That sound is of coal being delivered to your coalhole. The coalmen would slide the metal manhole cover off and pour sacks of coal down the chute. It would land in a pile at the bottom. Then we'd collect it as needed in a coal scuttle. Like that.' She indicated the one by the fireplace.

'We found that in the cellar,' I said. It was quiet now. 'I can tell by your face there's more to this.'

'There is,' she said. 'I was a teenager when we moved in next door, in the early 1960s. Everyone had coal fires, and we'd get sacks of coal delivered once a week. Quite a few of the houses round here still have their coalholes. You do – it's under your outside doormat.

And I've still got mine.

'Anyway, due to air pollution and smog making people sick – smog is a mixture of smoke and fog – the government passed legislation in the 1950s and 1960s to stop the public burning coal and make the air cleaner. Most of us got our fireplaces blocked up and had gas fires fitted.

'But something dreadful happened in this house before they blocked off the fire.'

Edith paused.

'You have to tell me,' I said, feeling shaky.

'A young couple moved in, like you and John, in the early 1960s. The girl was beautiful, elegant, but the man was brutal and bad-tempered. We'd hear them arguing at night, through the walls. They'd got wed because she'd fallen pregnant.'

A bit too much like our story so far, I thought. 'Carry on,' I said.

'Our coalman, Steven, was a casual labourer who helped out a friend or relative in the business – I'm not sure which. He was a handsome fellow. I remember because he used to make my heart flutter. It's no surprise Steven and Annie – that's the lady – began an affair. They'd carry on their business in the living room – this room. My mother saw them through the window once, kissing.

'But the husband found out. Annie and Steven weren't careful and he'd come mid-shift, covered in coal dust that he'd wash off in the kitchen sink. It was hard to clean linen properly back then, so Annie would hide his blackened towels in the cellar.

'Her husband worked out the day of their regular meetings and hid by the back door for the next one. When he saw Annie and Steven through the window, he kicked the door in and punched Steven to the ground. Steven's head struck the coal scuttle, then the fireplace. That one punch killed him.'

'What?' I cried. 'A murder in my living room?'

Edith nodded sadly.

'The husband, not knowing what to do, dragged Steven's body down the cellar steps and left him there. But he was caught and put in prison. Annie and the baby moved away.'

'I can't believe this,' I said quietly. Yet it all made perfect sense.

'Since then,' continued Edith, 'several families have

tried to settle here. Some stuck it out for a few years. I've never told any of them the story.

'But over the past weeks, I've watched you get thinner and thinner, and you look so mournful. I wanted to speak up. I feel guilty for not telling the others and giving them the chance to leave.'

John came in and Edith repeated her story.

'So we've lived in a genuine haunted house for a month,' he said, his mouth set in a grim line. 'I didn't tell you, Keely, but a few nights ago, while you and Tara were in bed, I was watching TV when I heard raised voices in the kitchen – a man and woman. They were arguing but I couldn't tell what they were saying. I switched off the telly and the rowing stopped.'

'Over the years, people here have reported all kinds of things,' said Edith.

'Maybe that coal bucket was the one the guy fell on,' said John. He put it in the garden, then came in and unzipped his rucksack. 'At last, I've got a powerful torch. I couldn't find my old one, so I bought this. I'm going to take a proper look at that cellar.'

He took out a large heavy torch and unlatched the cellar door. Tara had fallen asleep on the floor holding her teddy. 'Can you mind her?' I said to Edith. 'I haven't seen the cellar yet.'

Waving away John's protests, I followed him down the cellar stairs. The cold of it made me gasp and, as he reached the bottom, he took my hand to help me down the last few steps.

'Ah. There is a central light,' he said, directing the beam at the ceiling, 'but there's no bulb in it.'

The dank smell of soil and musty water was so overpowering I almost gagged. A strong sense of foreboding hung in the air.

As John shone the beam into each corner of the floor and ceiling, I clutched his shoulder. 'Can you feel – I can't describe it–'

'If you mean a kind of despairing horror, then yes, I can,' he replied.

There was a tiny window close to the ceiling, so filthy it let in almost no light. From its position I could see it led to our front garden, but it must be obscured by bushes, which is why we hadn't noticed it. Under it was the ancient chest of drawers and two large wooden crates John had mentioned. He'd put them back against the wall.

In the far corner, John's beam picked out what looked like an angled tunnel. 'The coal chute under the front door,' he exclaimed. We examined the brick lining, which was black with the dust, as were the nearby walls and floor. Damp coal particles seemed to seep into my skin.

'The coal hole will be at the top,' I said, coughing, as I took the torch off him and shone it up the chute. 'There – the circular manhole cover.'

As we looked at it, a sound began next to me. Very slowly, the top drawer of the grubby chest began to slide open.

'That's it,' said John, grabbing my hand. 'We're outta here.'

After we'd seen Edith off down the front path, John stooped to move the large doormat aside and there it was. Our brass manhole cover.

'I need to call my dad,' I said.

Shooing John into the back room, I got my dad on the phone.

Mum answered, but this was between me and my father. 'Dad,' I began when he came on, 'there's something going on in our house.'

There was a pause at the end of the phone. 'What do you mean, Keely?' he said uncertainly.

I described what Edith had told me and the things that had happened to us.

'I knew some of this,' he said eventually, 'but I thought it was just rumour. Then Tommo and Neville had a few problems during the renovation. Tools vanishing and reappearing in different rooms. Draughts and puddles of water where they shouldn't have been. Once they'd unpacked the floorboards for one of the rooms and came back after lunch to find every one had been snapped in half.'

He stopped. 'Anything else?' I asked.

'Well... that first day when you and John went upstairs and I was downstairs with Tara, I actually saw a man. He came from the hall, walked towards the cellar door and vanished into it.'

'You saw that and you didn't tell me?' I yelled. 'And you let us stay here with Tara?'

'Sorry, petal,' he said. 'Me and Grant have done up quite a few houses and we've come across a lot of similar disturbances. People walking through walls. Unexplained noises. From talking to other builders, so have they.

'And I didn't have another place for you and John. You'd been evicted and were desperate. Besides, John's a strong guy, so I thought you'd be safe with him.'

'From real-life threats, maybe,' I said angrily. 'But ghosts, not so much.'

'As it happens,' continued Dad, 'we've finished another place early. A flat this time, so no garden for Tara or your flowerbeds. It's a few streets away. You and John pack up and I'll get you moved tomorrow.'

And that's what we did.

Christmas in our new flat was a joy with our baby, surrounded by family.

Edith has become a good friend, but she understands that I can't bring myself to visit her, even though Dad has had the entrance to our old coalhole concreted over.

I won't walk past that house, although it's the quickest route to the shops.

Dad didn't rent the house out in the end. It's on the market and has been for the last year.

And Edith has promised to tell her story to anyone who comes to view it.

THREE
RAPUNZEL

The cosy festive hotel break Ellen had booked for herself and her young son didn't quite go to plan...

ALMOST A YEAR AFTER my divorce, as Christmas loomed, I felt guilty that I'd be depriving my seven-year-old son, Mack, of our usual family get-together with my ex-husband's parents. Mine lived in New Zealand and I couldn't afford to fly out so, in an attempt to make the best of a difficult situation for myself and Mack, I booked us three nights in a guest house on the south coast from

December 23rd to Boxing Day.

The small hotel looked lovely in the photos, with a huge Christmas tree outside, cheerful lights draped around the bushes and windows and a jolly inflatable Santa plus reindeer on the grass. The brochure promised crafts for kids, quizzes and board games, and we could stroll on the seafront if we wrapped up well.

I hoped the holiday would serve as a distraction for both of us, especially Mack, from the last miserable months of the break-up. It had been instigated by myself after some difficult years.

Now I wish we'd stayed in our house with our spaniel Piffle, who I'd left with my brother, and begun making new festive memories at home straightaway.

Mack and I took the train and as we climbed out of the cab in the hotel's drive, my heart dropped at our first sighting of the place.

The brochure photos were clearly several years old. Even in the fading light, the whitewashed outside looked dingy and neglected. A tree, much smaller than in the picture, had a few lights on and the ones looped along the windows hung low, dragging on the ground in places. Santa was there, but he and his sagging beasts could have done with a good blast from a pump.

I said nothing to Mack as we headed into the dimly lit hall, and, ever the confident boy, he dashed ahead, his footsteps muffled by the thick carpet, which had moth holes here and there. Suddenly, he stopped and turned to me. 'Mum,' he stammered. 'Look.'

Behind the reception desk sat a man in his thirties with cropped, dark blond hair and a prominent nose. He was grinning at us, and I was about to tell Mack off for pointing, thinking he was gesturing at the man, when I saw what my son was drawing my attention to. On the desk beside the receptionist sat a doll — an eerie, old-fashioned creature in an ornate lace dress, with oversized grey irises, painted-on spidery lashes and arched eyebrows, and long, Barbie-like fair hair topped by a lace cap. Standing, it would be at least 18 inches tall.

'Hello,' said the man cheerily, winking at Mack. 'I see you've spotted Rapunzel. She loves to greet guests as they arrive. I think she likes you.' Mack clung to me, his face buried under my arm, an uncharacteristic reaction for him.

I peeled him off and led him towards the man. 'She's lovely,' I said shortly. 'We're here for three nights...' I gave our names and filled out my details on the card the man, who told us his name was Jonathan Williams, had offered.

He turned to dig around in the cubby hole beside him that housed the room keys and I noticed the back of his head was unusually flat. Before I could take the key, the doll, which was seated on a blue satin cushion, plunged off the desk and landed at Mack's feet with a thud in the same stiff-legged sitting position.

He drew his toes back with a screech. 'She does that,' said the man benignly. 'Can you pop her back, please, Mack?'

Anger flared in my chest. Williams had already seen that my son didn't like the doll. Why would he push the thing off, knowing it would scare him? I was on edge as it is, having seen how tatty the place was. Did I really want to spend three nights in this place with such an insensitive host?

I opened my mouth to complain but before I could speak, an older woman emerged from a door behind Jonathan and gave us a tight smile. Retrieving the doll and placing it back on its cushion, she took the key from him.

'I'm Mrs Williams – Mary,' she said. 'I'll show you to your room. It's on this floor, just down the corridor.' She walked briskly ahead and we followed, Mack clutching my hand.

The room was drab, with two single beds and a scuffed wardrobe, and my heart sank even further. 'Sorry about my son Jonathan,' said Mary. 'He lost his granny, my mother, recently. She collected dolls, and Rapunzel was her favourite, her special girl. Jonathan took the loss of his gran hard, even though my mother never took to him on account of... the problems he's had since birth. She was often very unkind to him. Harsh lady, she was. But he was determined to have Rapunzel.'

She shot me an anxious look. 'Jonathan doesn't work outside of our hotel, and I don't want the doll in reception, but it makes him feel better if it's there and...' Mary trailed off and, sensing her embarrassment, I changed the subject. I understand the things one does for one's kids.

'Are there many other guests here for Christmas?' I

asked.

Mary shook her head. 'Fewer than usual. Cost of living crisis, I suppose. Maybe another... eight people? No other children, I'm afraid,' she said, looking at Mack, who shrank back.

After explaining about mealtimes and the festive activities on offer – not as many as I'd hoped – I saw her out with a heavy heart. Mack threw himself onto the nearest bed and buried his face in the pillow.

'Mum, I can't stay here,' he mumbled. 'Rapunzel was staring at me and she's close by, just down the hall. What if she comes to get me in the night?'

I sympathised with Mack and wanted him to have a nice time this Christmas, but I was starting to feel exasperated. I wasn't going to indulge this fantasy with the doll. 'Mack, why don't you unpack the toys you brought? You've got your car set and your wooden yoyo. Let's get them out.'

Mack remained face down. 'Mummy, I don't want to stay. Not with Rapunzel out there.'

I sat on the edge of the bed and stroked his shoulders. 'It's just a piece of plastic, and it can't hurt you. You're here with me, and I won't leave your side. Now, let's get unpacked and see if tea is ready. Mrs Williams said it will be in the dining room at six o'clock, and it's nearly that now.'

Mack did as I asked, and we stepped into the corridor. Unfortunately, to get to the dining room, we had to walk past reception. Jonathan Williams sat focused on his computer, his face illuminated by the screen, tinny voices and small bangs suggesting he was playing a computer game, the doll by his side.

As we got closer, I saw the doll's hair wasn't actually blonde. It was white and colourless, like that of an elderly person. I had a sudden awful thought. What if Jonathan had somehow put his dead grandma's hair on the doll? After all, they often have real hair... No. That was a stupid idea. And not a helpful one.

Mack was behind me and I heard him whispering, *'One, two, three, four.'* I turned to see he had both hands cupped on once side of his face to shield his eyes from the doll. *'One, two, three, four,'* he repeated. Grabbing his hand, I pulled him into the dining room. 'Mack, what is this?' I asked.

'Four will keep me safe,' he said quietly. 'Our room is number four. Four is here to help me.'

Inwardly, I sighed. He was back to the counting. This wasn't a good sign. It had started just after his dad had moved out to live with That Person, and I'd hoped it was behind us. I thought it best to say nothing.

In the dining room, there was no sign of Mrs Williams. I was going to have to talk to her about that doll. Yes, her son wanted it next to him in reception, but it was upsetting *my* son. And given that we were the paying guests, our needs should come first. But our meal was served by a girl and we didn't see Mrs Williams.

There were no other diners when we sat down because we were having an early tea for Mack. But within half an hour other guests began to trickle in, nodding to us in a friendly manner as they arrived in ones and twos.

Mack was given five chicken nuggets and slipped one onto his side plate but ate the other four, I had my spaghetti carbonara, and we went into the lounge. For the first time in hours, I felt my spirits lift. With wall lamps glowing a soft yellow, a real Christmas tree in the corner, its lights flashing pink, red and purple, and a fire burning in the grate, the room was calm and welcoming. Our hosts had made an effort indoors at least.

My son, looking a bit more upbeat after his tea, gestured towards a pile of games on the sideboard and we went over.

'Shall I teach you dominoes?' I asked, picking out the slim wooden box.

'No, here's a Buckaroo,' he said. 'Let's do that.'

We took the box to a table by the Christmas tree. Loading up the mule while it threw off its burden had him giggling after 20 minutes, which was a delight to see.

A different girl handed round mince pies and mulled wine, the latter, with its sweet cinnamon scent and the slight kick from the red wine, being so welcome I felt like relieving her of the whole jug. The other guests came in and as they murmured over their drinks, some chatting, others playing cards as Christmas songs played in the background, I felt my shoulders relax. This was what I'd wanted. Company, but at a distance.

Mack accepted an orange juice and I said nothing

when he carefully divided his mince pie into four with a fork.

Later, we rose to return to our room. Mack didn't mention Rapunzel, and I put myself in between him and it as we walked back. The reception desk was empty, apart from the doll.

We donned our pyjamas and settled into our beds. I put on the TV, we watched a talent show and by 10 o'clock, Mack's eyelids were drooping so I tucked him in and turned off the lamp by his bed. I kept mine on and read for a while.

It was snug in the room, even with the usual creaks and groans of an old house settling itself for the night, and I felt peaceful as I turned off my light and lay back. I could hear Mack breathing steadily in the other bed.

I must have been asleep for an hour when I was woken by gasps next to me. In the semi-darkness I could see Mack sitting up in bed. Still half in my dream, I groped for the lamp switch but couldn't locate it in the dark. Mack's gasping got louder, and then he let out a couple of sharp, high shrieks. It's a sound I'll never forget.

'Mack, what on earth is it?'

The temperature, warm and cosy so recently, had dropped so low my teeth began to chatter.

'Look at my feet, Mum!' he cried. As I watched, he pulled his knees up to his chest and hugged them to him over the coverlet.

'What do you mean? There's nothing there.'

He shot me a terrified look. 'Rapunzel was sat on my feet, then she reached under the cover to touch them with her hard cold fingers. She's at the end of the bed. You must be able to see her, Mum. You MUST!' Then he started to scream.

I jumped out of bed and went over, thinking he must be dreaming. But he was wide awake and seized my hand.

'She's there!'

'Mack, there is no doll.'

I pulled him towards me, but he let go of my hand and wrapped both of his around his knees again, drawing his feet in even tighter.

Standing by my son, I looked again at the foot of his bed. For a second, I saw stiff figure half-hidden in the gloom. The height of a small toddler, pale lacy dress, pale face, long pale hair, hands stretched towards Mack. Then it was gone, like a candle that had been blown out.

Gasping, I ran to put on the overhead light on and tried to get Mack out of the bed. He tumbled onto the floor, I hauled him up and we fell backwards onto my bed together. By now Mack was shaking all over, so I wound the duvet around us both and held him close.

'Mum, we've got to leave,' he said, jaw quivering. 'She hates boys and she hates me. She wants to hurt me.'

Unable to believe what I'd seen, I couldn't think what to say for the best. 'Is she still there?' I asked.

'No. Not any more.'

Then he said something no parent should ever have to hear. 'Mummy, I can't go on. Not with her nearby.'

I'd already decided we were leaving and explained that we'd go as soon as we could in the morning. I kept the lights on and read Mack one of his favourite stories until his eyes began to close and he dropped off, leaning against me. I nodded off too and was awoken early by him stirring.

'How are you feeling?' I asked.

He looked at me sternly. 'Mum, I haven't forgotten

about Rapunzel, I wasn't dreaming, and you said we could leave today. So please, let's go.'

We packed the bags, left the room and headed for the front door. Reception was behind us and I heard Mrs Williams call out. But I'm sorry to say that, hand-in-hand, we ran out into the street and down the road in the direction of the town, according to my glance at the map.

It was Christmas Eve. The town was a 15-minute walk and we ate breakfast in a fast food restaurant while I checked the trains home.

The journey to London took most of the day, but it was a huge relief to get back to the house. There was our little Christmas tree in the lounge with its baubles and tiny golden bells, lovingly hung by Mack just two days ago. The paper chains in red and green we'd made together were looped around the walls. Mack had attached a joke stocking for Father Christmas to the mantelpiece with sticky tape. It was about to fall off and he rushed over to reattach it.

I'd been watching Mack anxiously since we left the hotel but, astonishingly, he seemed fine. No counting, no mention of the doll, nothing about the number four.

A tap at the door revealed my brother with Piffle, plus several boxes of shopping.

On the sofa, Mack cuddled our spaniel and I cuddled them both. 'We'll have a lovely Christmas, just me, you and Piffle,' I told him.

'Mum, that's perfect,' he said, his beaming smile showing his missing front tooth. 'It's exactly what I wanted.'

I don't believe in the supernatural, so I assume that my sighting of the doll on Mack's bed was nothing more than my imagination working overtime due to my distress at seeing my child so terrified.

And I prefer to view the situation that way.

Four

The Second Bed

Ben's experience at the home of his girlfriend's parents left him a changed man...

THIS HAPPENED SOME YEARS ago when I was 28. I believe it was a case of possession. But you read my story and decide for yourself.

I'd been dating a Scottish girl, Moira, for a year and a half. For months she'd been dropping hints that we should get married, and I knew she wanted kids. I'd had a difficult childhood and wasn't sure about making such a big commitment, nor was I interested in becoming a dad. My parents were divorced and refused to speak to each other, which made life tough for me and my brothers, especially as Mum and Dad had both gone on to have more kids with new partners.

I'm from Liverpool, which is where I lived with Moira, and many readers will know that's a very specific accent, which is why what occurred in Scotland was so disturbing.

Moira and I were going to Edinburgh to stay with her family for the Christmas period. I'd managed to avoid meeting them so far and was anxious because I thought they might be checking me out to see whether I was husband material. I certainly didn't feel like husband material myself.

I knew her parents lived in a detached house they'd inherited from Moira's cousin a year ago. Not to be mean, but I was disappointed when our cab drew up outside a dingy brown pebbledash-covered building, yards from the pavement with a railing along the overgrown front garden. Her mum and dad greeted me warmly, though, in contrast to the inside of the house, which was very cold and draughty.

Moira hadn't mentioned this, but I don't think her family had much money judging by the dilapidated state of the house. They were obviously used to wrapping up warm rather than putting the radiators on.

Her parents were content to let us share a bed. Moira had only stayed in the house once before, in a room with a single bed. For our visit, they'd put us in the guest room.

'The double bed's not new, but it's comfy,' said her mother. 'You'll find the room a bit rough and ready, but you can light a fire in there if you like.'

In the large room, the bed nearest the door was made up but next to it a few feet away was a second double bed, the decrepit mattress bare. 'I don't like the look of those brown stains,' said Moira, wrinkling her nose, 'but Mum's done her best, so let's be grateful.' A built-in wardrobe with two doors was to one side and, opening it, we found a tasselled red cover that we threw over the second bed. 'There!' said Moira. 'We don't have to look at the stains, at least.'

It was Christmas Eve, and I took us for dinner at the local Indian. When we got back to the house, it seemed colder than ever, especially in contrast to the warm restaurant we'd just left. 'I'll put the heating on for an hour,' said Moira's dad, Ken. 'Do you want me to light the fire in your room? I'm afraid your radiators don't work.' We declined as I was worried about the smoke, so Moira took a fan heater up.

We sat by the log fire downstairs for a while, and I remember Moira's mother, Jean, with a pink blanket around her shoulders and a glass of whisky in her hand, laughing as she told us local stories. Ken kept our drinks topped up and provided a steady supply of snacks.

Even before the abnormal occurrences began, I found our room disturbing. We normally slept naked but, that first night, I understood why my girlfriend had urged me to bring my only pair of pyjamas. As we shivered in front of the fan heater, getting into our night things as fast as we could, I said, 'Moira, is there something wrong with this room? There's a feeling about it I can't identify.'

To my surprise, she said, 'To be honest, Ben, there has been talk about some kind of presence in the house. Not in here, though – on the top floor, above us. My sister says her son thinks he saw – I'm not sure what. Anyway, we have each other and we'll be fine.'

I cast a doubtful look at the second bed as we climbed into ours. Something wasn't right about it.

We chatted for a bit, then Moira fell asleep. I switched off the lamp but couldn't relax sufficiently to sleep. Fully awake, my eyes kept being drawn to the spare bed, which I could see dimly in the light from the streetlamp outside shining through the thin curtains.

Then I noticed muffled sounds in the room that I couldn't identify at first. I strained to listen and, gradually, I realised I could hear someone crying. It gave me goosebumps on my arms and, as I lay there wondering what to do, the crying ceased. I snuggled against Moira, taking comfort from her warm body, and did my best to sleep.

I was just drifting off when I started awake. The crying had begun again, louder this time. A child was sobbing and the noise came from the direction of the empty bed.

Often people say they were frozen with fear at such times. I wasn't. I knew I was awake, so I sat up and pressed the switch on the bedside lamp to turn it on. Nothing happened and the room remained in semi darkness. The sobbing continued. It was the most frightening noise I've ever heard before or since, and it made my blood run cold. This child, whoever he or she was, sounded in absolute despair.

As I said, I've never been paternal and wasn't keen on children. But this sound made my heart clench in a way nothing ever had before. My feelings were a combination of being very frightened because I was in the presence of something supernatural, and very sad for this child who was obviously extremely young and suffering terribly. Even without much light I could see the room clearly. There was no child there, nor, I assumed, anywhere in the house.

Then, alongside the desperate sobbing came a slithering sound. Movement on the bed caught my eye. The tasselled coverlet was slowly sliding off, as though dragged by an unseen hand.

As I heard the cover pool on the floor, a surge of emotion welled up in me and I found myself speaking. And, adding to my alarm, the words came out in a distinctly Scottish accent very different from my usual Liverpudlian one.

'Aye, hush noo, wee bairn, ye're all right,' I said. 'Yer da' is here. He'll take care o' ye.'

The sobbing stopped.

As I sat against the headboard, trembling and sweating, Moira open her eyes sleepily and raised herself on her elbow. 'What was that?' she asked. 'Did I hear you speaking in a Scottish dialect? It was so broad you sounded like my Granddad. What's going on?'

I tried the side lamp again, which, mercifully worked now, and explained about the child, showing her the coverlet from the spare mattress on the floor.

Moira began to get out of bed. 'Come on. We need to move rooms.'

I caught her arm. 'No, love. Let's lie here.' Incredibly, I'd gone from feeling sheer terror to experiencing a profound sense of peace. That last event had taken place in no more than 15 minutes, but I felt changed in a way that's hard to describe. Gazing at Moira on the pillow, her long auburn hair tousled from sleep, it was as if a veil had fallen away and I could see all her good qualities shining like a halo around her head.

That experience turned my commitment phobia into an urge to deepen my relationship with Moira. We slept in that room for the rest of our stay, during which I instigated conversations about our future.

I ended up proposing to Moira that New Year's Eve, in front of Edinburgh Castle. I even felt open to the possibility of fatherhood.

Me and Moira have been married for six years and we have two children, a boy and a girl. I'm glad I took the plunge as family life suits me, but I don't think I'd have done so without that terrible experience at Moira's parents' house.

Who was that child and the father he longed to hear from? Jean and Ken won't discuss the topic but, at some point, my wife and I will investigate the history of the house.

The thought of one of my kids enduring whatever pain and torment that ghost child had been through saddens me more than I can express.

FIVE
DEADBEAT DANIEL

***Peter's brother didn't believe spirits
could do you harm...***

THE EVENT I'M ABOUT to relate happened a handful
of years ago. My parents have an apartment in Spain
where they stay for winter as Mum swears the warm
weather eases her arthritic hips, meaning she can
delay the inevitable hip replacement operation. They
normally come home for a family Christmas, but
this particular year Mum's hips were so painful they
decided to stay overseas.

Fortunately, my brother Rory, a doctor, had bought
a house in Gloucestershire six months ago, near his

job, so I arranged to stay with him for the week. I was 22, had recently finished college and was working in a call centre while I decided what to do with my life. Living with my parents, I was happy to stay home alone while they were away as I had a ton of mates. But they'd be with their families over Christmas, so Rory's invite was most welcome.

Rory, who lived with his near-silent girlfriend, Bernice, was collecting me from the station. He was alone when he pulled up in his silver Ford Puma. 'Bernice is at home getting the house all festive,' he said. 'I've told her she has to speak to you and make you welcome. So let's hope she can manage that.' Bernice had joined him a few weeks ago.

His terraced house was bay-fronted, with jaundiced yellow paintwork and double gates that led to the garage at the side.

'Get out would you, Pete, and open the gate and garage door so I can drive straight in,' said my brother. I did as he asked and he parked the car while I waited outside. At the back of the garage was a chest freezer and a cupboard.

'I thought you said you had a big kitchen,' I said as

he beckoned me inside.

'I do. Big as a barn.'

'Why do you need a freezer in the garage, then?'

Rory laughed. 'For my hobby. Leave it alone, though. You don't need to worry – no human skulls in there.'

I scowled. Such a patronising jerk.

My brother had always been an oddball, studious and good at school, which made me feel like a dunce, not that he or my parents ever said so much or even hinted at it. But he never got less than an A in his exams and my Bs and Cs felt like failure in comparison. No doubt his success had contributed to my feeling lost and confused in terms of my life direction.

From the garage, we entered the house through a door that led into the kitchen and I left Rory to unpack the shopping while I wandered around the ground floor. I'd never been here before, although I'd met Bernice a few times over dinner and hadn't managed to find out a single thing about her from her own lips. She was 21 and had met my brother at the coffee shop where she was a barista, near the GP practice where he worked.

In the back living room behind the kitchen, Bernice was assembling a large artificial Christmas tree, slotting branches onto the spine. Boxes of new decorations sat nearby.

Bernice was very shy and looked up briefly through her fringe to flash me a small smile, shaking her long, afro-type hair. 'I like these,' I said picking up a box of glass ornaments representing London landmarks. A golden Big Ben, a black taxi, a silver and blue tube train, and a guardsman, in his black glass bearskin and red jacket.

'Let me help you do the tree,' I said.

At one point, she gave a small gasp but when I glanced her way, she shook her head and carried on unpacking the glittering star for the top.

It looked great once we'd finished and Rory brought a ladder so he and Bernice could attach the red crepe bells and white snowmen to the beam that ran across the ceiling.

He sent me to the kitchen for more tacks. 'Still doing your paintings, bro?' I called from the hallway. There were several framed watercolours of birds:

pigeons in groups, a blackbird on a branch, three robins on a fence. The detail was superb. And I got a pang of envy. Yet another talent my brother had that I didn't – art.

'Yeah,' he replied, distracted as he and Bernice arranged a pine bough over the mantelpiece.

Meanwhile, you probably won't be surprised to hear I was determined to sneak off and look in the garage freezer. Leaving by the back door, I crept up to the freezer, even though Rory couldn't hear me from his location. Stood in front of it, I hesitated. Rory was five years older than me and as well as being a science nerd with a gift for art, as I've said, my brother was quirky, and not always in a positive way.

When I was little, he thought it hilarious to show me terrifying paintings of Hieronymus Bosch devils to make me cry and he'd trick me into watching frightening films. Once he made me sit through the found-footage horror movie *Paranormal Activity* and wouldn't let me out of the room until the end. I was only 10. And I swear my heart almost stopped with fright at the last scene, which I won't describe in case you haven't seen it.

So you can understand why I had to look in the freezer to see what Rory was up to even though I was worried at the thought of what I might find. I willed myself to get on with the task and just open it. The lid was stiff, so I tugged and pulled and finally lifted it up.

Arranged neatly in baskets were bird corpses in plastic bags, of all things, arranged by breed. A pile of blackbirds. One full of sparrows. Quite a few pigeons. A lone magpie – *one for sorrow*, I thought. Even, which I found sad given the season, a couple of robins.

The moment I clocked what I was looking at, I slammed the lid down before I had chance to take in what state the bodies were in. I didn't want to see any blood or nastiness.

But my brother knew me well and when I slunk into the kitchen, he could tell from my face that something was wrong. He was washing his hands at the sink. 'Did you enjoy my bird collection?' he asked, grinning at me over his shoulder. 'I knew you'd look.'

'I wouldn't have bothered if you hadn't told me not to!' I blurted out.

'Yeah, I know that,' said Rory, drying his hands. 'Reverse psychology. Don't worry. They're roadkill –

I'm not mean enough to dispatch the birds myself. I'm all about preserving life, not taking it. I'm a doctor, remember?

'Every one of those creatures was found in the road. Better I took them than the foxes. They're fantastic for getting the anatomy correct in my artwork. Leonardo Da Vinci used to dissect animals for the same purpose.'

I wasn't so sure about it being better that Rory had the birds, but I decided to put my feelings of disgust to one side. I was here for Christmas, Bernice was nervous enough as it was without me and Rory starting one of our feuds, and I didn't want to ruin things by sulking. Even though my brother was, to be honest, a bit of a shit.

I went upstairs. The bathroom was at the top, to the left. Then there was what was clearly Rory and Bernice's room, then the dumping room, with exercise bikes, cases and whatnot. Opposite the bathroom was a small room with a single bed, which was mine for the week. The bed faced the door and at the end of it was a low cupboard and I slung my rucksack on the top.

As I did so, something small rolled out from underneath the bed and hit my foot. It was a red toy bus made of metal.

I must have disturbed the floor walking on it, I thought, picking up the bus. It was cool, so I sat it on the cupboard next to my rucksack.

Next stop, lunch. As I walked down the stairs, I saw a figure slip past into the kitchen, too fast for me to get more than a fleeting impression. My heart racing with alarm, I quickened my pace to the bottom and rushed after it.

The kitchen was empty and I could hear Rory and Bernice in the back room.

'Oh, who did I see then?' I said to myself. That's when I knew. *Forget it, Pete*, I thought. *Leave it.*

Now I need to tell you something, which is that I've always been sensitive to the supernatural. All my life I've seen and heard things I can't explain and to be honest, I hate it. Some call it a gift. I call it a curse and I wish it would go away. So when I spotted the figure, the familiar crawling sensation around my scalp told me that maybe this wasn't Bernice or Rory, and maybe there was *something* in the house. Rory would take the mickey out of me, as per, if I spoke up. That's why he'd always got a kick out of scaring me – he'd heard my tales before. This time, I wasn't going to say anything.

We passed a quiet Christmas Eve, although Bernice and I were forced to sit through one of Rory's horror films – *The Exorcist*. I sat to one side of them so I could keep my eyes shut through most of it. Bernice kept covering her face with her hands, so wasn't enjoying it either. *One of us should find the courage to stand up to Rory*, I thought.

The next day, Christmas Day, we all helped cook lunch, even Rory, and had a surprisingly pleasant meal, pulling crackers, telling the silly jokes that came with them and donning the paper hats, with even Bernice laughing when hers ripped and fell into her Christmas pudding, thanks to her big hairdo.

Afterwards, stuffed full of turkey and roast potatoes and in something of a food coma, we settled down for festive TV in our paper hats, with Bernice daring to suggest that we take turns to pick the programmes.

During a break from a game show, my choice, I nipped to the loo. Even before I pushed the door open

I had a bad feeling. There, sitting on the pan, was a man aged around 50, trousers around his ankles, with a broadsheet newspaper open in front of him, the lower edge resting on hairy thighs. With the ruddy complexion of someone who liked a drink, he was in profile, wiry curls threaded with grey, his equally grey eyebrows knitted in concentration. He looked perfectly normal but, as I stood transfixed in the doorway, the man turned to look at me.

As if I'd been in any doubt he wasn't human, his eyes made it clear. They were white, just white, with no pupils or irises, like boiled eggs. He turned back to his newspaper and I galloped down the stairs so fast I tripped on the bottom step and went flying into the living room.

'There's a man in the bathroom!' I shouted. I described what I'd seen and my brother chuckled, although Bernice looked on the verge of tears.

'No,' said Rory, 'there's no man in the bathroom. I think you've just met Deadbeat Daniel. We see him in the house occasionally – or, that is, we see shadows. And he moves objects around. But thanks to your so-called psychic connections to the spirit world, it sounds like you may have had had a full-blown encounter.'

I stared at them. 'But why on earth was he on the toilet?'

'Because he died there,' replied Rory. 'A surprising number of people die from a cardiac arrest on the loo. They have a weakness in their heart, they're straining to push out a poo, then bang!' he slapped the sofa arm for emphasis and Bernice and I jumped. 'The heart stops beating and they're dead. Doesn't help that they're alone and have often locked the door. By the time they're found, it's too late. That was Daniel's fate.'

'Like Elvis,' whispered Bernice.

'Yes, the Constipation King thanks to an endless diet of cola and cheeseburgers,' said Rory.

'Forget Elvis,' I said. 'What about your ghost?'

'I guessed when I bought the house that it was "haunted", in inverted commas. The estate agent who showed me round told me the last owner keeled over on the toilet the previous year. The agent hated his employers and planned to leave, so he was telling everyone this tale so they wouldn't buy the house and line the estate agent's pockets. He explained about Daniel, a bus driver and a miserable man according to neighbours, to several other prospective buyers and they scuttled off fast. But I laughed, because I don't care.

'I'm not frightened of ghosts, especially Deadbeat Daniel,' he said, raising his voice for the latter half of the sentence to mock the apparition.

'Well, I'm scared of them,' I said. 'You know I've seen things I've struggled to deal with. Like Auntie Jill in the hallway after she died in an accident. And those soldiers in a field in France. I get nightmares after. For days and days.'

'You don't need to worry about Daniel,' said Rory. 'I doubt you'll see him again. Actually, I doubt you've seen him at all because you've always imagined things. You probably read something about his death in a newspaper and forgot.'

Then Bernice spoke quietly. 'I see him every day, and I don't like it. I won't stay here on my own. He follows me about the house.'

'Ah, that's why you go to your mum's while I'm away,' said Rory, not very sympathetically. I couldn't understand what Bernice saw in my brother. Other than him being handsome, well-off and a doctor... pah.

Prior to tonight, I hadn't seen anything other than the shadow and the bus trundling out from under the bed, which I now assume was Daniel's doing.

But I was worried at the thought of going to bed given that the bathroom where he'd died was directly opposite my door. How could I visit the loo in the night knowing a ghost might be in there? Would he enter my room?

We continued with our Christmas Day, FaceTiming Mum and Dad while Bernice rang her parents, but I felt agitated and I could see she was uncomfortable, too.

The day wore on, the shadows deepening outside the windows, and I needed to go upstairs for my headphones. I flicked all the lights on, planning to be in and out of my room within seconds. Grabbing the headphones, I turned to leave when something struck me painfully on the back of the neck. On the floor was the metal bus. Daniel had thrown it at me. There was no other explanation.

Cursing, I rubbed my neck, but the room was silent. Maybe he'd gone. As I gathered my courage to leave, I heard soft footsteps on the landing by the stairs. I held my breath. Someone was creeping towards my room. Panting outside the door in gasps told me they'd arrived. Muscles tense with fear, all I could think of to do was press myself against the wall behind the door, which was ajar.

It was pushed open.

There stood Bernice. She was crying.

Then she spoke at length, longer than I'd ever known her to. 'I was in the kitchen slicing the cake just now when something grabbed my shoulders and started shaking me like I was a rag doll,' she said through sobs. 'Last week the marble bread board flew off the kitchen island and hit my knee. And when you and I were decorating the tree yesterday, I'd just taken a purple bauble out of the box when it was snatched out of my hand, then it vanished in mid-air...'

'Ah,' I said, putting an arm around her as it seemed to be required. 'That time when you gasped?'

'Yes. But whenever I mention any of it to Rory – well, he does think there's a presence in the house, but it doesn't attack him like it does me. It's probably scared of him.' She began crying harder and I got the alarming impression she was scared of my brother, too. 'He brushes it off and tells me everything's fine.'

Something in me snapped. 'We're going downstairs,' I said firmly, 'while I have a word with him.'

I led the way, Bernice behind me. I was halfway down the stairs as she stepped onto the top tread when there was a thud, followed by her scream as she pitched down the steps. She hit me, I overbalanced and we tumbled down the rest of the stairs together.

Rory appeared, helping Bernice to her feet and ignoring me. 'Don't tell me you're as clumsy as my brother,' he said, giving her cheek a playful pinch.

I swatted his hand away and stood next to her. 'I think I know what just happened. Bernice?'

'It was all so fast,' she began, wiping her eyes, 'but a shadow came through the wall by the bathroom and I got pushed down the stairs.'

'No you didn't,' said Rory. 'You tripped over that loose bit of carpet on the landing. Whatever's in the house – if there *is* anything – it can't hurt you. Ghosts don't behave like that. They don't assault people, whatever the ghost hunters say.'

'Maybe I did trip...' she began. I cut in. 'Daniel is here and he does hurt people. He grabbed Bernie in the kitchen earlier. I reckon he did push her. He's certainly capable of it.'

Rory sighed impatiently. 'Let's change the subject. Why don't you make a start on the Christmas cocktails, Pete? The stuff's out in the kitchen.'

Exasperated, I turned on my heel and headed for the kitchen as Rory muttered in Bernice's ear. I heard her draw away to look at him. 'What?' she asked.

I stood out of sight to listen. 'I said "There goes Pointless Pete,"' said my brother. 'That's what I call him behind his back. He's hopeless in every way you can think of.'

To cut a long story short, I stormed out and let rip with the home truths about Rory I'd kept to myself for years, while Bernice called her dad and asked him to fetch her.

With no transport on Christmas Day, I had to stay one more night, sleeping on the sofa, before I could get a taxi next day.

Bernice dumped Rory and, a few months later, we began dating. She's gentle and lovely and we're now baristas in the same coffee shop, well away from my brother's neighbourhood.

I'm not speaking to him, although I probably will in time. But I know from my parents he's still in that house. I hope Daniel's making his life a misery.

Six

MISERY LOVES COMPANY

*Iris found the ideal flat – apart from an area
in the corner that never got warm...*

ONE WINTER 15 YEARS ago, I moved into a
ground-floor flat with its own front door, quite old,
Edwardian maybe. I didn't like the fact the front door
led directly into the living room, but the place was
cheap and as a girl of 26, it served my needs. Towards
the back were two bedrooms, a bathroom and a galley
kitchen.

I found it hard to relax in the front room, for

reasons I couldn't explain. It felt draughty by the big bay window with its curved alcove, even with the thick charity shop curtains I'd hung up. An area in the corner, in between the window and fireplace, was always so chilly it sometimes felt like you were stood in front of an open fridge.

A rubber plant I put there shrivelled up within days and had to be thrown out, and the floor lamp I replaced it with gave me such trouble with the bulb blinking on and off that I moved it to my bedroom, where it worked perfectly.

I thought perhaps there was damp in the wall, or holes in the floorboards underneath letting the wind in, but the builder sent by my landlord said the place was sound. My best friend Fay, a Canadian with no family locally, was coming for Christmas and howled with laughter when I mentioned how uneasy I felt in my lounge.

'I guess if someone burst through the front door while you were watching TV you'd have no time to escape,' she said with a wink.

'Thanks, I hadn't thought of that,' I said grumpily.

'They'd grab you, tie you up and ransack the place

within minutes!' she continued, nudging me to make me laugh. I wasn't amused, though. It was a few days before Christmas and we stood facing the bay window, each cradling a coffee, while we decided where to put the tree.

'The market down the road sells real ones,' said Fay. 'You have the ideal spot there, in the corner by the window. With a plug socket for the lights we're definitely going to buy. Along with the tinsel and as many ornaments as we can carry from the discount shops. Lovely and tacky, heaving with bad-taste decorations!'

'No,' I said, 'the tree can go on the other side. I'll move that chest of drawers.'

But when I got home from work two days later, Fay, who had time off, had a surprise for me. Hearing my key in the lock, she darted forward, putting her hands over my eyes as she led me into the flat, saying, 'Don't look yet!'

We stopped but, feeling the draught around my knees, I knew where I was standing.

'Vulgar, but amazing!' she said, taking her hands away. Fay had put the tree in the wrong corner but, with tiny white twinkling lights almost hidden by a covering of silver tinsel as heavy as a winter coat, red plastic hearts and mirrored cubes peeping out and reflecting the lights, I had to laugh at how absurdly overloaded the poor tree was. 'Got it all today and sorry, but that was the best place for the tree. You like?'

'I like,' I said with a sigh. Another sigh came straight after mine, quieter but unmistakable, and Fay looked at me. 'It's not that bad, is it?'

Perplexed by what we'd both heard, I said, 'Of course not. You've done a great job. I'm just tired. The boss worked us extra-hard this week as the office will be shut for a while.'

In the kitchen sorting my laundry later, I considered the events in the lounge.

Something had felt unsettled in the house since I moved in, but I hadn't seen or heard anything out of the ordinary other than that sigh. I'd been here two months. How could adding a Christmas tree make things worse? And what was it about that corner? I had wondered whether there was something wrong with the plug socket, but the tree lights were working fine so far. I'd keep an eye on them.

It was Christmas Eve, and we'd bought each other some jokey presents to unwrap the next day. My bedroom was by the lounge, Fay's next to mine. We watched some festive telly and, as midnight rolled around, both rose to go to our beds. 'Happy Christmas, honey bun!' I said, pressing my cheek to hers. 'See you Christmas morning!'

'Same to you and have a fab festive sleep,' she said.

We'd drunk quite a bit of wine, and I woke in the night needing the bathroom, which was several steps from my room, past Fay's and towards the back. As I turned into the hall, the lounge behind me, I heard another sigh at my elbow. I turned swiftly. I was alone, but I felt a shiver run through my body. An unmistakable sense of unease hung in the air.

After the loo I walked back, planning to return to bed. Yet something told me to continue to the lounge. I didn't want to, but my feet carried me there without me being able to stop them and as I approached, I heard a faint rustling.

We'd turned off the tree lights before going to bed, but there they were, twinkling away underneath their blanket of tinsel. Next to it stood a child in a white nightgown, hands hidden by the tinsel, which it was feeling around under. It turned as I entered, a candy cane in its fingers.

At first, it looked like a normal child, then I realised the figure was glowing unnaturally, as though illuminated from the inside. A boy, with delicate features, brows knitted together, his sad eyes about to spill tears down the thin cheeks.

Normally I'd feel moved by such a sight, but here, sensing the child wasn't real, wasn't actually alive, terror rather than pity rose in my throat. My brain couldn't compute what to do next so I had no choice but to remain where I was, gazing at the spirit.

And suddenly, it wasn't there anymore. Then I heard that sigh, this time ending in a muffled sob. The striped cane lay on the floor.

My heart was hammering. Should I wake Fay? I needed her sensible take on what I'd experienced.

I didn't knock on her door. Instead, I burst in, and she sat up in bed, instantly awake. 'What on earth's the matter?' she asked. 'You –'

'Don't say I look as if I've seen a ghost,' I said, 'because I think I just have. A little boy in the lounge by the Christmas tree.' I told her how he'd looked, the sadness, the sigh I'd heard earlier and just now.

She looked troubled. 'Do you know, when I was dressing the tree, a couple of times I felt something tugging at my jumper, like someone trying to get my attention. And it is strangely chilly in that corner, isn't it?'

'I hadn't mentioned it, but yes, there is something unpleasant about that area, which is why I didn't want the Christmas tree in it.'

Fay was in a double bed, so although it felt silly at my age, I climbed in with her and we managed to fall asleep.

Next morning, we padded into the lounge together. The Christmas tree was on its side, the tinsel in bits on the sofa, the lights pulled off, and the few gifts we'd left under it had been thrown across the room.

'Well, whoever that child is, it didn't like the Christmas tree,' said Fay. 'This is madness. What can we do? We can't stay here.'

'I'm not having my Christmas ruined by a – a non-entity,' I said. 'Let's put the tree back, for a start.'

We did our best to re-assemble the tree and gathered

the presents, which luckily hadn't been damaged. Then we tried to put the events to the back of our minds, eating the smoked salmon breakfast I'd bought, opening our gifts, and listening to festive tunes as we roasted a chicken for lunch.

But with all our efforts at normality, I could see from Fay's face that she was uneasy, and I couldn't settle. Walking around the flat, I kept thinking I heard light footsteps behind me but, when I turned, no one was there.

Not knowing what to do with ourselves, we thought about going for a walk, but the day was too icy for that to be enjoyable. Later we went to the local pub for a few gins and didn't want to leave at chucking-out time.

But with nowhere else to go, home we went. On the doorstep, I said to Fay, 'Right, I've had enough of this. I'm going to deal with it.'

'How?' she asked, entering the lounge behind me.

'You'll see.'

Taking off my gloves, I faced the Christmas tree. 'Look,' I began. 'I don't know who you are, but I'm sorry you had an awful life. And an awful Christmas.

You must have done, otherwise, you wouldn't be here. But please don't bother us. We'd love to help you, but we can't. Please, I beg you, go away.'

A red glass bauble detached itself from a lower branch of the tree, landed with a gentle plop on the carpet and rolled to my feet. The certainty of what that meant swept over me. 'He's gone,' I said, stooping to pick it up. 'This is his peace offering.' I placed the bauble on the mantlepiece by a plaster Father Christmas with a sack over his shoulder.

The only way I can think of to describe what happened next is that it felt like the sun coming out after a violent thunderstorm. In the room, the atmosphere lightened, and a sense of tranquility seemed to settle around me.

'Go you, Iris!' said Fay. 'I'm impressed. I think that worked.'

Even so, neither me nor Fay wanted to be alone that night, so we shared her bed again. Both of us were restless and, expecting crashes in the lounge or worse, I stayed alert for anything untoward. But the flat remained quiet and, eventually, I slept.

In the morning, Boxing Day, the tree looked a bit

bedraggled, the tinsel hanging lower than we'd left it but, other than that, nothing had been disturbed.

After that, Fay and I relaxed, and the last few days of the holiday were uneventful. In late January, she came to live with me at the flat, which pleased me as we got on well, plus we'd shared an experience no one else would understand.

From the day I asked the spirit to leave, the corner became the same temperature as the rest of the property. Lamps placed there continued to work and plants stayed alive (unless neglected by us).

Fay is still my best pal, but we've long since gone our separate ways, gathering husbands, kids and the like. Only occasionally do we refer to our old flat with its lonely little ghost and wonder whether he appeared to subsequent occupants.

Seven

I Hear You Knocking

***Francine had everything ready for
Christmas with her father...***

This is the oddest thing that has ever happened to me and it was incredibly distressing.

My husband Kevin and our two teenage daughters, Jade and Gerry, were out doing some last-minute Christmas shopping and I was home alone, taking advantage of them being gone to wrap their gifts.

The day before Christmas Eve, I sat on the rug in the upstairs spare bedroom surrounded by boxed presents, reels of ribbon and packs of wrapping paper, trying not to get carpet fluff on the sticky tape as I bundled up gift after gift.

It was late afternoon and I planned to get as many finished as possible before my widowed dad arrived at 6pm to spend the holiday season with us.

Being December, the night was black outside the big window above me, the curtains open. I'd prepped the room for Dad yesterday and looked forward to him being with my family for Christmas, knowing how sad he was – desperate at times – after the loss of his wife Effie nearly a year ago. Effie hadn't been my mum – she'd died of cancer when I was in my twenties – but Effie had been kind to my dad and at the age of nearly 70, he missed her like mad and wasn't doing too well on his own. I adored my father, who'd been a huge support to me when my first marriage broke down.

Me and the girls and Kevin had got him a new laptop for Christmas, alongside other treats, and planned to show him how to get online so he could chat to his brother in Australia.

I was folding star-spangled paper over his gift when

I heard a knock on the door. 'Damn!' I thought, looking at my watch. 'That'll be Dad. He's so early – it's only 5pm. Guess he must be bored at home, so it makes sense. Annoying though – I've lost an hour's wrapping!'

I threw my scissors and tape aside and bounded down the stairs. As I reached the front door, another knock rang through the house, the person on the other side banging the brass knocker with force.

'Hang on, Dad, don't break the door down!' I called, releasing the catch and pulling the door wide. We have an enclosed, double-glazed porch with an outer door to the front garden. That door had been slid to one side, showing the concreted-over space where we parked the car, currently empty as Kevin had it. No one stood on the doormat in the porch but I couldn't see how anyone could have sprinted away that fast after the almighty knocking – I'd opened the door a second after the last round.

Grabbing my key so I didn't get locked out, I ventured onto the concrete in my slippers, feeling the chilly ground through the thin soles, and to the iron gate. The night was dark, the street silent as I glanced up and down it. Not Dad then. Kids, maybe, having a laugh? It was so cold though. I shuddered in my thin jumper, rubbing my upper arms as I walked to the house, slid the porch door shut and closed the front door behind me. Time for more present wrapping.

I had a foot on the first step of the stairs when I heard a sound from the lounge to my right. I strained to hear. Nothing. About to continue upstairs, the sound came again from the lounge. Inside, I put on the light at the same moment I heard the noise for a third time. The wooden window blinds were folded back, the inky sky visible beyond, and the noise came from that direction.

Now I recognised it.

It sounded as though someone had slapped the glass with an open palm. A palm, or something hand-sized and wet.

I went to the window. Light from the room illuminated the immediate area outside, the further reaches of the garden towards the low wall in shadow. To the left, I could just make out our two dustbins, their silver lids and sides gleaming in the light. As I watched, a shadow emerged from behind them, solid and tall. It moved slowly towards the window as I looked on, fear beginning to rise in my chest.

The black mass stopped several feet from the window and I couldn't work out what was in front of me. Shadows aren't thick and dense, like black smoke, yet this seemed to be. What felt like long minutes passed.

The spell was broken by another knocking at the door, forceful and insistent.

By now, my heart was in my mouth. Should I answer it? What if it was something to do with the shadow?

I shook my head and, as I did so, I realised the black column wasn't there anymore.

Rap rap rap!

Trembling now and leaving the light on behind me in the lounge, I cautiously eased the front door open, bit by bit.

A figure stood on the porch doormat, inches from me. I saw an arm, a shoulder, then –

'Dad!' There was my father, smiling uncertainly. I laughed, relieved. 'You've given me such a fright. I thought you were an intruder, creeping about in the garden.'

Dad continued to gaze at me, his brow furrowed in a perplexed expression. His wavy grey hair was wet, swept away from his forehead, the black winter coat he always wore at this time of year glistening with moisture, as though it was sopping.

'Is it raining?' I asked with a joviality I didn't feel. The night was frosty, but I couldn't see any rain behind him. This was weird. 'You're all soggy! Come in and get warm.'

I stepped back to let him pass, glancing down at my slipper as I did so. It had come loose, and I manoeuvred it back onto my foot. When I looked up, Dad had gone – and the porch door was still firmly closed, as I'd left it when I'd come in.

I slammed the front door, numb with shock initially, my thoughts scrambling over one another. Then I burst out crying and sat on the stairs weeping and wondering what to do. 'You idiot!' I thought. 'Ring your dad!'

I raced up the stairs to my phone, scrabbling around the floor and eventually locating it under the sheets of paper and tissue.

Seven missed calls from my sister, Irene. As I held my phone, about to listen to her voicemails to stall for time as there was clearly going to be bad news, it began to ring. Irene again.

'Where have you been?' she yelled. 'Dad had a stroke during his walk by the pond this afternoon and fell in. A couple of dog-walkers dragged him out and called an ambulance but there's been a lot of brain damage. Get to the hospital – quick. I'm on my own with him and the doctors don't think he'll wake up.'

Well, Dad didn't wake up and died a few days after Christmas. Dr Frome, his consultant, said Dad had suffered so much brain damage and swelling that his quality of life would have been poor indeed, so although we're desperately sad, Irene and I think that quietly fading away was the kindest outcome for him.

I told Irene about my horrible experiences the day of Dad's stroke and that somehow, I'd 'seen' him after his fall in the pond, dripping wet and confused as to what had happened to him. 'I've read about crisis apparitions,' I said to her, 'where people appear to loved ones at the moment of death or a serious accident.'

Irene, who's an occupational therapist and very practical, hugged me and said, 'Francine, if that idea gives you comfort, then so be it.' I can tell she doesn't believe me.

I wonder if there's some envy there because Dad chose to visit me in his final lucid minutes and not her? I wouldn't tell her that, though.

EIGHT

ONE LAST HOLIDAY

Initially, Sara was happy to stay in a different hotel from her colleagues at their work conference...

IT WAS A FEW days after Christmas and I wasn't happy about being torn away from my family, but I had no choice but to attend a two-night work conference with six other employees in the north of England. We were all to have rooms in the same hotel.

According to the pictures I found online, the hotel was in a pretty village, and I drove up with my friend Maisie. When we arrived just after 10am, the other five plus our two managers were already there. While we were having coffee, the hotel owner came over.

'Your rooms are ready,' he said, 'but I'm afraid we've had a bathroom flood in one and we don't have an extra room as it's the holiday season and we're very busy. My brother owns the hotel down the road and he has a room free...'

He wanted a volunteer and, as I'd noticed the hotel he was referring to when Maisie was parking the car and it looked particularly cheerful and Christmassy, the doorway flanked by a pair of pine trees with red bows, that I offered to go. It was only for two nights, then I'd be home to my husband Ray and our three children. A welcome break from all that festive cooking, if I'm honest, but I would miss the kids.

I said my goodbyes to my colleagues and set off with my case to the second hotel. A youth showed me up to my room, number 11. It wasn't what I expected. Curtains in burnt orange, a patterned carpet to match, and a double bed. A sprig of faded plastic holly sat in front of the TV.

I got the impression the suite had been prepared hastily as the yellow coverlet was rumpled and pulled away from the pillows, while the three mustard cushions that I assume were normally arranged in front of them had fallen to the floor.

Slightly suspicious, I sniffed at the pillows to check the bed hadn't been slept in. They smelled of lavender soap powder, fresh and clean, so I tidied the bed up, stowed my case on a leather chair and walked the few minutes to the first hotel.

Morning and afternoon meetings had been arranged in the hotel's conference room, dull discussions about the housing association I worked for. I popped back to my room after lunch to grab a new notepad and change my blouse.

The ensuite, which I hadn't paid much attention to when I'd thrown my toothbrush and toothpaste on the sink, was surprisingly old-fashioned for a modern hotel. A bath, sink and loo in sickly bubble-gum pink with a red carpet – ugh. Carpets in bathrooms always got soggy and I was glad that had fallen out of favour. The room and bathroom were like something from the 1980s.

Oh well. It was clean enough and fine for a couple of nights. The afternoon meeting was about to begin, so I returned to the main hotel.

After more PowerPoint presentations, we had dinner and cocktails and I felt very merry indeed by the time I made my way back to my room.

The foyer was quiet, and I was still chuckling at one of Maisie's stupid jokes when I opened my hotel room door with the electronic key card. The bed was to the left as you came in, and initially I hesitated in the doorway, thinking I must be in the wrong room.

There in the bed I could see the top of an elderly man's head, gleaming in the light coming through the doorway from the hall, with white strands of hair across the bald scalp. The curve of his shoulders and body showed he was on his side towards me, although his face was hidden by the bedclothes.

The man stirred in his sleep and I withdrew, feeling panicky. But as I went to shut the door, I looked again at the number on it. Eleven. This was *my* room. So *he* was in the wrong room.

As the man was obviously very old, I wasn't sure what to do. I knew this hotel was also packed for the holiday season.

Anyway, my things were in there, so I decided to

go into the room, creep around the bed and snatch my bag, which I hadn't unpacked apart from a few toiletries, from the chair.

Why I didn't just go back to reception, I can't say. Probably because I was a bit drunk and not thinking logically. I pushed the door open just wide enough for me to slip in, but as silently as I could so as not to disturb the bed's occupant.

However, the bed seemed to be empty. My palms sweating, I slipped my key card into its slot by the door that controlled the electricity, and the lights came on.

Yes, there was no one in the bed, although the cushions were back on the floor by my feet and the coverlet was disturbed again, even though I knew I'd straightened them both before I left.

My heart raced as my mind started conjuring all sorts of paranormal scenarios. 'Oh, come on,' I chided myself, trying to stop my unease from escalating. 'It's just your imagination.'

Telling myself what I'd seen in the bed was an unfortunate combination of the arrangement of the four pillows at the head of the bed, my three mojitos and the slit of light from the window, I pulled my night things on and climbed into the bed on the other side from where I thought I'd seen the man. Amazingly, I fell asleep immediately.

Next thing I knew I was woken up by the feeling of weight pressing down onto my ribs so hard I struggled to breathe. Then, even worse, I felt something soft come down over my eyes, nose and mouth, rendering me blind and suffocating me at the same time. Pressure on either side of the mass suggested someone was pressing a pillow onto my face with their hands, and the person appeared to be sitting on my ribs.

Terrified, I tried to thrash my hands on the bed but I couldn't move them as something – knees? – had pinned my arms to the mattress. Opening my mouth, I couldn't scream due to the cushiony mass filling it.

I must have blacked out because when I came to, to my surprise, it was morning. The details of my horrific experience the night before came rushing back and I got up, dressed as quickly as I could, packed my bag and rushed over to the main hotel for breakfast with my colleagues. We had another full day's events planned but all I wanted was to go home to my husband.

Speaking to my colleagues over scrambled eggs, I began to feel calmer. Maybe I could stay on for the last day if the hotel owners gave me a different room, preferably at this hotel rather than the one I'd stayed in. If not, I was definitely leaving.

In the first meeting, though, I couldn't focus and during the break, Jenny, one of the bosses who I'd known for years, approached me.

'Bad night's sleep?' she asked. 'I actually saw your hands trembling earlier when you were writing and you're as pale as rice pudding!'

I'm a timid person who doesn't like to make a fuss, so I wasn't sure what to say. But Jenny asked more questions and eventually I blurted out what had happened to me the previous night, thinking I saw a man in the bed, followed by the feeling of being suffocated.

Rather than treat me like the foolish person I felt myself to be, she patted my hand kindly. 'I believe you,' she said. 'Wait there.' I could see the hotel manager outside the glass doors talking to another guest and Jenny marched up to him. The other guest moved away and I watched as Jenny appeared to be having a heated discussion with the manager, who was shrugging apologetically and looking shamefaced.

Then she returned, her expression a mixture of worry and annoyance. 'I told the manager what you described, and he said there had been a dreadful incident in the 1980s in your room – number 11. It's generally kept locked because several other guests have had similar experiences to you in there, and it hasn't been updated along with the rest of the hotel. But he said the luxury suite here has become available as the couple in it left due to an emergency. He's offering it to you for the night if you'll agree not to mention the incident if you write a review of the hotel.'

I really wanted to leave, but I said I'd take the suite as I had my position in the company to think of. 'Yes, OK,' I said to Jenny. She looked very uncomfortable. 'I get the impression you know what happened in that room,' I said. 'Please tell me.'

Jenny frowned. 'An elderly couple came to stay and, according to their daughter, who came from her home in the Caribbean to see the room after the event, her parents adored each other. But they were both sick, the man with stomach cancer and the woman with lung disease. The wife was very anxious that she might die before her husband, as there was no one else to look after him and she knew he couldn't bear to be left in a care home.

'She told her daughter she wanted her husband to have one last good holiday while they were both still mobile.

'The couple had a lovely few days at the hotel, according to the staff. Then, on the last night, the woman killed him with, er, a pillow, presumably attacking him in his sleep. But afterwards, she must have been overcome by guilt, as well as realising she'd most likely go to prison for his murder. So she swallowed her sleeping tablets, along with some of her husband's medication, and was found dead on the floor next to the bed.

'Very sad tale.

'The bed the man died in was taken away after the first time a guest experienced something – she saw two ghostly figures on it, apparently – so it's not the one you were in. It's in the same position though, because there's a plug socket on either side for the lamps.

'The room hasn't been used in years, but the hotel

was full so our manager's brother had it made up for you as a favour. It was hoped so much time has passed that any unpleasant, erm, residue would have faded away. But it seems not.

'It will be shut up for good now.'

Although I'd had a dreadful fright, I was still alive, unlike that poor couple. To have committed such a terrible act, the woman must have felt the kind of despair I can't begin to imagine.

That night, in my suite, I said a prayer for their souls. I hope they've found peace together.

Nine
Testing Times

No one looks forward to medical assessments, but Hazel's experience was quite out of the ordinary...

THIS HAPPENED SEVERAL YEARS ago and was extremely disturbing.

It was a few days before Christmas, and I was off to hospital for an investigation. I'd had pains in my belly area for months, but I wasn't overly worried because I have what you might call a sixth sense, and it was whispering to me that I'd be fine.

Also, my best friend Molly was a nurse at the

hospital – in the department next to where I was visiting, as it happened – and we were going for an early dinner, which I looked forward to as we hadn't had a proper catch-up in ages.

I got off the bus and, during my walk to the hospital, even though the weather was freezing and my teeth were clenched against the cold, I couldn't help but admire the snow. It dusted the bushes, formed a layer on top of the post box like a white hat, and blanketed the bench I passed outside the hospital's sliding doors.

As I approached the department, there was Molly, pushing a tray of instruments along the corridor. We greeted each other and I must have looked a bit apprehensive because she squeezed my arm and said, 'It's not that bad, honestly, and you'll be out within half an hour.'

'I'm fine, really,' I said. We confirmed where we'd meet later and I carried on to my section.

After giving my name and address to the receptionist, I turned towards the waiting room, groaning as I took in the rows of full chairs. 'The doctor is only two behind, so it'll be you very soon,' said the receptionist. 'Take one of the corridor chairs outside and she'll call you.'

I sat on an orange plastic one and was the only occupant on the bank of five seats. After a while, the receptionist popped her head around the corner. 'You're on in 10 minutes,' she said with a smile. 'Quarter past four.'

Although I hadn't been worried initially, as my appointment time approached, I began to fret, unable to concentrate on the free newspaper I'd picked up on the bus. Would the procedure hurt? I'd just folded the paper to put back in my bag when I heard the squeak of wheels to my right in the corridor.

A male orderly in a navy uniform and a Santa hat was slowly pushing a trolley with a person on it. I say a person, but a white sheet veiled their feet, which stuck up, and, as the trolley came closer, I saw the whole body was covered – including the face. *Oh my goodness*, I thought. *I can't believe this man is pushing a dead body through the hall in front of me.*

Feelings of sympathy for the dead person swept over me. Then, as the top end of the trolley was a yard away, the body under the sheet began to sit up. It didn't go all the way, though, like in a horror movie.

Rather, its head and shoulders lifted a few inches from the bed through the sheet and I saw a man in profile, middle-aged but haggard, with wormlike grey lips and a shockingly pale face, a kind of greenish glow about him.

Shocked, I watched as his head came level with mine, although he was a foot or so higher. Slowly, the face turned in my direction. The man's eyes bore into mine as he shook his head sorrowfully before casting a look past me towards the department I was due to enter.

Then I found myself looking at the corpse lying flat on the gurney under its sheet as it passed, the orderly going on his way as though nothing had happened, which, from his point of view, I guess it hadn't.

I sat blinking with shock as the pair continued down the corridor. And then I thought, *I've got to go, I've just got to go.* I stood up and, without telling the receptionist I was leaving, ran to get the bus, slipping on a patch of ice near the post box and hurting my ankle so badly I should have gone back to the hospital, which had an accident and emergency department. Instead, I struggled home, my jeans chilled and sodden from my fall in the snow. No way was I returning to the hospital today.

By now, it was rush hour. It took me nearly an hour to get home, and I was almost in tears from the trauma of what I'd seen plus the pain of my ankle. My phone kept ringing as I hobbled to my house. I knew it was Molly, but she'd have to wait.

Falling through my front door at last, I plucked my phone from my bag and punched in Molly's number. 'Where on earth did you get to?' she asked. 'I thought we were meeting straight after your procedure.' I told her what had happened, and she suddenly became distracted, which annoyed me as I was pouring my heart out. 'Hang on,' she said. 'I'll ring you back in a sec.'

I was on the sofa with a bag of frozen peas on my ankle when she rang. 'Bloody hell, Hazel,' she said. 'There was a problem with the machine you were about to have your scan on. It malfunctioned and a patient was badly burned. You had a lucky escape. Maybe the dead man you saw was telling you to leave so you wouldn't be injured. Assuming he *was* dead...'

I didn't repeat his description. No point.

I found this most peculiar. How come I was warned not to get the scan, but the girl who got burned wasn't? I'll never know, but I'm grateful I saw a ghost that day.

TEN

NO SMOKE WITHOUT FIRE?

Forced to take the train to see his folks one Christmas, Teddy's experience put him off rail travel for life...

THIS EVENT TOOK PLACE several decades ago.

It wouldn't have happened if my car hadn't needed mending. And maybe it definitely wouldn't have happened if I hadn't taken my dog Caleb on the train with me.

My Mini had failed its MOT and I had no choice but to leave it in the garage over Christmas while they made the necessary repairs. The outrageous cost meant fewer gifts for my parents, sisters and cousins, who I was to visit for the festive period, but so be it.

I hated train travel. The trains weren't the clean, safe vehicles they are nowadays. Smoking was allowed, and even the non-smoking carriages smelt of cigarettes because plenty of smokers ignored the signs, not to mention the angry glares of other passengers.

And rather than today's electric doors that glide open and shut at the touch of a button, at that time, train doors could only be opened from the outside, by sliding down the window, leaning out and turning the handle, risking getting your head bashed off as the train went into a tunnel if you weren't paying attention.

Caleb, a cross between a Dalmatian, a greyhound and a mountain goat, if his ability to shin up rocky paths was anything to go by, was a well-behaved boy, used to lying patiently on the back seat of my car on journeys. So I knew he'd be no trouble on our trip to my family a couple of hours' train ride away.

We ran through the icy drizzle and jumped on a bus to the station. On the platform, I juggled my rucksack, a bag of wrapped gifts and Caleb's lead. Enjoying the unfamiliar sights and smells of a railway station, he dragged me along the platform with such enthusiasm it was hard to assess the carriages to find a no-smoking one containing as few people as possible and preferably no dog-haters.

During my flight down the platform, I spotted a compartment with the red no-smoking sign on the window that looked empty. Hard to imagine now, but some carriages were self-contained cars spanning the whole width of the train, with a long seat along each of the two walls and a hand-operated door at either end. The only way out was to the platform via one of the doors, so if you needed the loo or were stuck with a lunatic, potential rapist or would-be murderer, you had to wait until the next stop to escape.

It was a few days before Christmas and my train was at 10.30am, too late to be crammed with commuters and, I hoped, too early for the holiday flight out of London. Gratefully, I unlocked the carriage door and threw myself in after Caleb. Yes, empty. I took the seat facing the direction we were travelling in.

Rather than place my bag of presents on the rack

above my head and risk them falling off and braining me if the train stopped abruptly, I put it on the far side of my seat, duffle coat around my shoulders and my rucksack on the other side.

Caleb settled on the seat by the door we'd come through and sat on his haunches to gaze out of the window, nose close to the glass. I know you're not supposed to let dogs on the seats, but he was my beloved boy, used to sitting with me on the couch at home, and I imagined he'd enjoy watching the scenery flash by. The window above the door on the left side didn't close fully and a draught blew through, making me shiver every now and then, but it was worth it to be alone.

I'd brought peanuts and a bottle of orange for myself and treats for Caleb, and we were content, just the two of us, as the train rattled along. I found the rhythmic movement and gentle swaying so soothing that I leaned back to savour it rather than taking out my newspaper. The buh-dumph of the wheels, annoying at first, added to this and I found my eyes closing.

It took an hour to get to the station from my

house and last night, I hadn't slept well as I'd been worried about missing the train. The rain fell more heavily now, pattering against the windows, a few drops coming through the gap in the left-hand one.

Content, that is, until half an hour in, we stopped at a small country station and a woman stepped into our compartment, bringing a blast of wintry air with her. Even before I took in her appearance, my nostrils curled at the smell of smoke that clung to her clothes, so strong I felt sick. *I bet she had a cig before she got on*, I thought. *If she dares light up, I'm going to give her hell.*

The woman gave me a half-smile that didn't meet her eyes as she sat down in the corner furthest away from the door she'd come through. It was chilly in the carriage and, rather than taking off her shapeless tweed coat, she unbuttoned it, leaving the edges together over her bolster of a chest. A small handbag with two looped handles lay in her lap.

She turned to the window, which gave me chance to study her unnoticed. While her face was that of a woman in her forties, her bushy mop of white hair, old-fashioned spectacles and thick neck with its heavy chins gave the impression of someone 20 years older. Her narrow lips were stained red, as though she'd applied lipstick hours ago and worn it away on a series of teacups.

Droplets of water slipped through the door window and dampened her knee, but she paid no heed to the wetness. Suddenly, still facing the window, she said, in a clipped, BBC newsreader voice, 'Stop staring. I'm not blind. And get that dog off the seat.'

Caleb looked round at me, as though he knew he were being talked about, then returned to his window-gazing.

This person had invaded my carriage, and I wasn't going to be kind. 'You could clearly see him through the window before you got on,' I said. 'Why didn't you pick another carriage if you don't like dogs?'

'I didn't say I don't like dogs,' she said, turning to look at me. 'They shouldn't be on train seats. It's wet out and his feet are grubby. What about the next person who sits on that seat?'

My cheeks grew hot. That, at least, was true, but I was so used to mucky paw prints around the house I hadn't noticed. Without replying, I took a pack of tissues from my bag and swabbed each of Caleb's paws as he licked my hand, before tackling the daubs of mud on the blue checked seat.

Next, my dog curled up on the seat and I reached over to position his speckled head in my lap. Planning to shut the woman out, I closed my eyes and stroked Caleb's head from his long snout to his floppy ears, over and over.

There's something odd about that woman, I thought, as I caressed Caleb's silky head. *But what?* I opened my lids a slit to peep at her. Her eyes were on me, brows knitted in a hard expression, but, noticing me looking at her, her gaze slid away to focus on the backrest to my left.

The rocking of the carriage and clattering of the wheels no longer made me feel safe and cosy. Outside, the wind had picked up and, thanks to the woman, the atmosphere in the carriage had grown oppressive. As I frowned with my eyes shut, pondering the situation, the woman gave a sigh. I heard the snap of her handbag opening, rustling as she felt around inside it, and the sound I'd been dreading: the striking of a match, followed by the smell of tobacco.

But I was drowsy and didn't seem able to open my mouth to admonish her. A minute or two passed, my hand on Caleb's head. He was asleep. Then I became aware of soft sounds, like the shuffling of shoes on the floor. Next, the whiff of cigarette smoke became overpowering and my eyes sprang open to find the woman standing over me. She was breathing heavily, eyes huge behind her magnifying spectacles.

'No. Dogs. On. Seats!' she hissed, holding the cigarette between finger and thumb lit end first. Then, with a quick movement, she went to jab it into Caleb's flank. My reflexes kicking in, my hand shot out to grab her wrist before she could touch him. 'You crazy– ' I began to shout – but my hand closed over empty air.

No woman. No cigarette.

We were alone in the carriage and Caleb snoozed on, emitting his familiar rasping snores.

Feelings of rage and disgust mingled with fear as my heart banged painfully against my ribs. No one touched my boy with anything other than love. *Ever*. But who or what had been in the compartment with us for the last hour? I thought back over that leg of the journey. I hadn't been aware of us pausing at other stations and I knew there were several more stops along the way.

Caleb hadn't paid any attention to the woman, not even glancing her way as she entered the carriage. If she were some sort of supernatural entity, wouldn't he have barked (not that he barked very often), or indicated in some manner that something was wrong?

She'd looked decidedly retro, but not in a cool way. Her glasses were the style I'd seen in photos of my great-granny Ada from the 1950s, like cat-eyes, pointed at the top outer corners, and her creased tweed coat looked like a jumble-sale find. Had I slept through and imagined her?

Caleb stirred, his brown eyes on me as the train drew into our station. My dad, on the platform in his hat and mac, waved a gloved hand and grinned as I gathered my things and took Caleb's lead.

'Good journey, son?' asked Dad, after opening our door.

'I'm not sure,' I started to say as Caleb pattered around excitedly on the carriage floor before jumping down the train step. Something clung to one of his back feet, dropping to the platform as my dad took the bag of presents from me.

It was a fresh cigarette stub, stained red around the filter, strands of tobacco spilling out the other end where it had been flattened by my dog's paw.

***

Old Caleb is long gone but I still miss him, even though I have a boisterous Lab called Donald. And I won't catch the train these days unless absolutely necessary. Which, luckily, is never.

ELEVEN

UNDER THE YEW TREE

A new house, job and boyfriend would have been great for Jessie if it hadn't been for what lurked beyond her garden...

ALTHOUGH WHAT I'M ABOUT to relate was frightful and has stayed with me, the event also stands out because we had a white Christmas that year, which is unusual, and the snow plays a part in my tale.

I've always had experiences that can't be explained by natural means, although they were most frequent when I was under 10. In the house I grew up in, I'd pass a child who wasn't real on the stairs every now and then, sitting on the landing halfway up. I couldn't see him when I looked directly, but if I squinted and peered to one side, he was there. It made me shudder.

From my bedroom window, I'd see a big brown dog, an Alsatian, I later discovered it was called, wandering around the garden from time to time. In summer he'd dig in the patch at the back behind our swing which was full of thorny blackberry bushes. You couldn't get into the garden without going through the house and we had no pets. I was aware he wasn't of this world.

My gardener dad left the area alone but, one summer, he cleared the brambles with my uncle John so they could extend the lawn and plant roses. I was there when they found the skeleton of a large dog in the ground. They re-buried it in the corner, but after that I didn't see the Alsatian again.

I'd hear whispering in the kitchen while getting a glass of milk after tea when no one else was there. My brother and sister never experienced any of this, nor did my parents.

What I'm about to tell you came much later.

As I've said, once I reached 10 or 11, the weird experiences stopped, apart from the occasional one. A decade on, I got my first proper career job in Newcastle, near college. My friend Kate, another graduate from my course, got a job in the same company. Excited to start the training scheme together that autumn, we did some house-hunting and found nothing. Then I went on holiday with my family for two weeks while she continued looking.

She found us a house while I was away, cheap and not far from the new offices.

'The only issue, Jessie,' she said to me on the phone, 'is that it backs onto a graveyard. Does that bother you?'

Hearing this, I had one of my shudderings, as I called them, that sometimes came over me before something spooky was about to happen. But I pushed the sensation down when I heard how much of our new wages we'd have left to spend every month if we took this house.

'Two of the new company recruits also want to live there. They're guys – and they're cute,' she continued.

'Come on,' Kate urged as I hesitated. 'It's a steal. Are you in?'

'Yep,' I said. 'I'm in.'

Because I wasn't there for the house viewing, I had

no choice but to take the room at the back no one else wanted. It overlooked the graveyard and when I peered out that first day as Mum and Dad helped unpack my boxes, my heart lurched when I saw an Alsatian darting through the gravestones. But then – relief! – a man ran behind it, shouting and waving a lead which, when he caught up with the animal, he clipped onto its collar before leading it out of sight.

Smiling, I turned away. Not my childhood dead Alsatian, then. Mum and Dad still lived in that house and I hadn't seen anything ghostly there for years.

We took the house for September, when the training scheme began, and it turned out to be quite a party palace. The two guys, Ezra and Arun, were indeed cute, and the four of us quickly became two couples who spent our free time together.

The graveyard wasn't discussed much and I barely noticed it, apart from the odd occasion that I glanced out of the window. Everyone kept their own room for their stuff although we couples shared a bed in one or other of them.

It wasn't until late October that I decided to take a proper look at the graveyard. 'Come on,' I said to

Ezra, my boyfriend, one Saturday morning. 'Time to examine our back garden extension.'

He agreed, and we walked the few minutes around the cemetery perimeter to the entrance. I pushed the creaky metal gate with its sign, *No Dogs Allowed,* and in we went. *Naughty dog walker I saw on my first day,* I thought as Ezra and I strolled over the stone flags and past the tall church with its green door.

The day was frosty and the white grass stood stiffly, like a carpet of tiny knives, with gravestones dotted around, stretching hundreds of yards on either side.

I felt content as my new boyfriend and I threaded our way through the headstones hand in hand, stopping here and there to read an inscription. Some stones had the top half broken off, while others leaned backwards towards the ground.

'Am I just morbid or is this romantic?' asked Ezra, stopping me under a tree and kissing my neck.

'Maybe that makes us ghouls, but yes, it is,' I said, laughing as I ran my hand across the thick, ridged trunk of the tree. 'Is this a yew? I read all burial grounds have them.' I rested my back against it and we kissed, his warmth welcome in the cold of the day.

Then one of my shudderings came over me and I stopped. 'This is disrespectful to the dead, Ezra,' I said, taking his arms from around my waist.

He pulled me close. 'Sod them,' he breathed in my ear, planting a kiss on the lobe. 'What are they going to do about it? Rise up and complain?'

At that moment, a woman's scream sounded in my other ear, so piercing I gritted my teeth against the pain of it. 'Ahhhh!' I cried, clapping both hands over my ears as I shook my head.

'What's wrong?' exclaimed Ezra, taking my hands away.

'You must have heard that,' I said, my shoulders trembling. 'A scream, long and high. Like a woman in a horror film. A mixture of misery and utter fury.'

He waved a hand. 'Nope. Lovely, peaceful silence, apart from the odd bird tweet. The dead sleep, Jessie. No one is screaming.' He went to kiss me again, but the romantic mood had been shattered for me.

Seeing my worried expression, he smoothed my furrowed forehead with his fingers. 'If there are any ghosts here,' he shouted, 'then just sod off! You're scaring my girlfriend. Back to your graves you go.'

'Let's just leave,' I said, heading for the path between the plots.

We were deep into the graveyard, the exit some distance away. Ezra caught me up and we walked towards the gate.

Was that the sound of footsteps in the grass? Someone following the path we'd taken in between the stones, just out of sight, yet almost parallel to us? I glanced behind me. The space was empty of life, except for a few sparrows.

Ezra was animated, chattering away about the Saturday night we'd planned at the cinema with Kate and Arun, but I felt uneasy.

And I was right to, because this was the day my difficulties in the new house started. How something as innocent as a smooch in a graveyard could cause so much trouble, I don't know.

In my bedroom the graveyard, from the window, was quiet and still, just as we'd left it. Then my heart lurched. The spot where Ezra and I had kissed and I'd heard the enraged, anguished scream was directly opposite my bedroom window. If I'd had a powerful catapult, I could have shot a marble to land in the exact spot. I knew where it was, because a grave marked with a tall cross, which I'd been only dimly aware of at the time, stood to the right of the tree I'd had my back against.

My attention was drawn to a sound at my elbow. On my desk sat a few trinkets I'd bought to go on our Christmas tree. Six glass baubles in a box, each with its own compartment, were visible through the clear lid. One of them, green with painted blobs of glitter, was spinning as though being twirled by an unseen hand, rubbing against its cardboard confines, which was making the noise. The lid flipped open, the bauble jumped out onto the desk and exploded, sprinkling shards of green glass on the desk and floor.

The other ornaments in the box began to shudder and dance but, before they could explode, I screamed, fled my room and ran down the stairs. Hearing me yell, Ezra met me halfway up.

'Jessie! What is it?' I described what I'd seen and, leaving me shaking on the step, he ran up to my room. Minutes later, he was back.

'The green ball is smashed all right,' said Ezra. 'Are you perfectly sure you didn't drop it?' He patted my cheek and grinned.

My jaw tightened. This was too much like what I'd heard every time I'd told Mum, Dad, or my brother and sister about a supernatural occurrence at home.

'You must have imagined it.' 'Nothing's there.' 'I think you're just tired.' Et cetera, et cetera. So I stopped telling them, and I wasn't going to say any more to Ezra.

'Quite sure,' I said. 'Let's make coffee.'

Nothing else odd happened that day, apart from finding my fashion magazine open flat in the centre of my bedroom rug when I knew I'd left it in my bag downstairs.

After that, in the build-up to Christmas, there were lots of silly things. A bottle of perfume was emptied over my pillow, making it so unbearably pongy I threw the thing out.

My pot of hair gel got smeared across my bedroom mirror when I'd been alone downstairs with the product, newly purchased, in a carrier bag by my feet. I found the empty pot upturned on my floor. A snow globe I'd brought from home ended up stuck base-first on my ceiling; we didn't have ladders so I couldn't get it down. It fell off and struck my back while I tugged my socks on one morning.

Ezra was never in the room when this stuff happened, and I was often alone in the house. It definitely wasn't my housemates pranking me.

Also, I often sensed what I can only describe as swirling fury in the air in my bedroom. Usually we stayed in Ezra's bed. I avoided looking out of my window, just in case.

Then, with Christmas days away, we were all thrilled one afternoon when the snow began to fall. We had drinks that night and Ezra and I collapsed into my bed.

When I awoke next morning, I opened the curtains to find the garden and graveyard covered in a blanket of white snow. The trees were frosted white, the headstones surrounded by snow that decorated the tops. The scene was beautiful and I gasped. Then I gasped again as I noticed the hood of my dressing gown had been ripped off in the night and hung over the edge of the windowsill onto the radiator.

'What is it?' asked Ezra, joining me at the window. 'Wow. Excellent. Let's go out after breakfast and make a snowman in the graveyard.'

'How about we do that in the park?' I said, rubbing my chilled hands together. 'That's only 10 minutes away.'

'It'll be more fun in the cemetery,' he said, hauling on his jeans.

Throwing the torn hood into my laundry basket out of sight, I thought about the situation. Ezra was sweet and playful, but he could be insensitive.

Since the exploding bauble, I hadn't told anyone about what had to be poltergeist activity. Anyway, it only took place in my room.

Ezra and I hadn't been to the graveyard since I'd heard the scream and the footsteps coming after us.

The four of us had planned to visit a Christmas market in town at lunchtime, this being another Saturday.

'Those two are still in bed,' said Ezra. 'We've got some time to play around before they get up.' Ezra didn't do lie-ins and had so much energy I could hardly keep up with him.

The churchyard did look gorgeous so I agreed, donning my wellies, padded coat and woollen gloves after our toast. 'It's so quiet it feels like we're the only people in the world,' said Ezra as we set off down the silent street. 'Look – ours are the first footprints of the day on the pavement.'

We walked along, marvelling at the trail we left. In the cemetery – not that I saw many people there when I dared to look – of course ours were the only footprints and I steered Ezra away from the area where I'd been screamed at a month ago.

Excited by the snow, we giggled like schoolkids as we rolled snowballs, throwing them at each other, and I soon forgot my apprehension, even when some of our white missiles struck gravestones and burst apart.

'Let's make a snow headstone,' said Ezra. 'A little one, before our gloves get too soggy.'

'What a weird and disrespectful idea,' I said loudly, foolishly hoping the graveyard ghosts, guardians or whatever lurked here understood that I was thinking of them, even if my boyfriend wasn't.

'Says she, giggling like a three-year-old and chucking snow around a cemetery,' said Ezra, slapping a snowball on my back.

'Quickly, then,' I said, 'before our hands freeze off.'

We set to work, fashioning a thick, 3ft tall headstone with a curved top, patting the front and back to flatten them.

Finally I was smoothing the top, facing the direction of the awful scream, when my eyes caught movement ahead and I glanced up. From 200ft away by the tree, something was heading our way. White and bulky.

Moving slowly.

I stared, trying to work out what it was. The thing seemed to be a hideous combination of mist, snow and white cloth in the shape of a head, narrow shoulders and a body, the height of a person.

Letting out a yelp of shock, I took a step back and tripped over a protruding stone, landing on my bottom in the snow. 'Careful,' said Ezra, reaching out to help me up. He had his back to the white mass, his looming form hiding it from my sightline. 'You'll get a wet bum as well as soggy hands.'

I got to my feet, fearful of what I might see, but I couldn't stop my eyes searching for the thing. Everything was so blank and white and still it was difficult to discern anything unusual.

Then, ahead, something moved. Something white, bulky, almost translucent. And as my eyes alighted on it, it became motionless again.

Just a tree stump, with snow clinging to the top and sides?

Except as I looked harder, the mass had two small, circular, black holes that could be eyes and a black slash underneath, where a mouth might be. Strands like hair hung from the head area.

'What are you staring at?' asked Ezra, turning.

At that moment, the gravestone we'd made flew to pieces, as though kicked by an unseen foot. Ezra's eyebrows shot up.

'Something's here with us,' I whispered, nodding in the direction of the white mass. It seemed closer.

'That tree stump?' asked Ezra, confused.

I gawped. He could see it! Or he could see *something...*

But where was it?

We looked at each other, then at the vacant space. 'Where'd it go?' asked Ezra, starting off towards what was now a gap between the graves. 'A walking tree stump. That's a new one.'

Not wanting to be left alone, I gave a little cry and ran after him, alert for any movement around us, especially a further appearance of the mass.

Instinctively, we headed for the tree where we'd kissed all those weeks ago. Now I saw the wide canopy of branches as protecting the sleepers below.

Under the tree, I told Ezra about the strange things I'd experienced since our first trip here. 'I'm struggling to believe those were supernatural events,' he said slowly, his frown telling me he also thought, *And I'm struggling to believe they happened at all,* 'but I love you and want to support you. What can I do to help?'

'I have a feeling this grave by the tree has something to do with it all,' I said, approaching the cross, which was carved with entwined fruits and leaves. I brushed the snow off them, then bent to clear the inscription.

It was bitterly cold standing there, but we had to do this. My intuition told me so.

'It's a woman's grave – no, a girl's,' said Ezra. 'It says, "Sacred to the memory of Lucy Burton, died 10 September 1924, aged 18."'

'Lucy was three years younger than me when she died,' I said. 'We were in her territory. We should have treated her final resting place with respect. But we didn't. We were snogging and you shouted at her. That upset her.'

I could see Ezra wanted to laugh but forced himself to keep a straight face. 'You think?'

'I do. Maybe she'd never had her first kiss, because she was only 18 when she died. Different customs then. No time to find love. Maybe it was hard on her to witness us together like that.'

Ezra sighed. 'If you say so.' He faced the grave. 'Lucy, I apologise for telling you to... go away, and treating you with a lack of respect. I'm sorry.'

I beamed at him. 'Can we go now?' he said, patting my shoulder playfully.

Back home, I knew my room would feel lighter, and so it did, the heavy oppression that was often present in the air since our first graveyard visit completely gone.

We spent a lovely Christmas in the house, just the four of us, and, although I did experience some odd events – in the rest of the house rather than my room, such as the TV switching itself on – they felt friendly, rather than threatening.

That was several years ago. Ezra and I didn't last, although we're friends, and I have a new partner. Marcellus believes in the supernatural and has had experiences himself. In fact, we've had some together.

But I'll save those stories for another time.

TWELVE

JOY

Rosie had information about her grandmother's death – but how...?

IT WAS EARLY NOVEMBER when two young policemen knocked at our door to tell us my gran had been killed in an accident. Aged 48, her motorbike had collided with a lorry under a bridge, and she'd died at the scene.

An unconventional lady, she'd had my mum when she was 17 and never told Mum who her dad was. My mother had been more like the parent in their relationship. 'I begged her over and over to ditch that motorbike and get a nice car,' sobbed my mum when the police had left. 'I had a feeling she'd go early and here we are.'

I wept too while my dad comforted us both with hugs. I'd just turned 13 and, with no siblings, me, Gran and my mum were so close that, for me, we almost felt like sisters. My mum was only 31.

Gran, whose name was Joy, had spent the weekends off from her job as a pharmacy assistant on meetups with her biking pals, who had get-togethers in pubs, cafes and umpteen biker-friendly hangouts. Every now and then I'd come into our kitchen to find Granny Joy talking animatedly to a hulking guy in motorbike leathers with oil-rimmed fingernails, while my mum made them endless cups of tea, tutting as she boiled the kettle.

Mum and Dad had me young, too, but they were still together, whereas Granny Joy had what my mum called 'a revolving door of unsuitable boyfriends' over the years.

A few weeks on it was time for the funeral and Mum insisted I accompany her to the funeral parlour where Granny Joy was. I didn't want to look at her face.

But after peering into the casket herself, Mum said I should.

I knew Granny Joy had been smashed up pretty bad and I was frightened of what I might see.

'The mortician did a great job covering up Mum's injuries,' said my mother quietly from her place by the casket. 'You can see her face and hands and she looks... peaceful. Come on. Have a peep.' Mum held out her hand. 'Otherwise, you might have nightmares about her appearance. I think it's best this is the last picture you have in your mind of Granny Joy, rather than your imagination working overtime and producing something horrible.'

I started at this. Since the accident, I *had* seen Granny Joy in my dreams, on the ground, her face contorted with pain. I hadn't told anyone apart from my best friend, Leila. I'd heard Mum and Dad talking, saying Granny's leg was torn off in the collision and she bled to death. The man driving the lorry had held her hand while they waited for the ambulance. It had been too late to save her.

Every time I had the dream, I saw a slightly different version of what I'd heard. Granny Joy was always screaming in agony while I floated several feet above her, unable to do anything to help.

Sidling over to the coffin, I looked in. I expected my gran to look like she was sleeping, but instead she seemed like a dummy version of herself with too much make-up on, her face an unnatural beige against the white satin of the casket.

My gran never wore make-up, apart from pink lipstick sometimes. I'd seen a TV programme on how the sculptors at waxwork museums made models of celebrities, and how the resulting figures look like them but a bit wrong, somehow. It was the same with Gran. Her face was serene, composed, whereas in life she was such a lively person, always giggling and bouncing around and cracking jokes, that I couldn't square this expressionless creature in the coffin with the person I knew.

'Her hair's too tidy,' I said. 'And she has what look like stitches on her top lip. Ugh.' My gran's short black hair was brushed neatly away from her face. It usually stuck out in all directions because she'd just pulled her helmet off.

'They probably stitched her mouth shut,' said my

mum, dabbing her eyes with a tissue as she placed Gran's red and black leather biking gloves on her chest. 'That's normal, I think.'

We said our goodbyes to Gran, then Dad, who worked as a driving instructor, arrived to drive us home.

The funeral was hard on all of us. Afterwards, the next task was clearing Granny Joy's house so it could be sold. And getting through Christmas without her.

My gran normally came to us for Christmas Day, often bringing her latest unsuitable boyfriend, so she didn't put up much in the way of decorations in her own house. One thing she adored, though, was candles and she had them dotted around the house, in various jars and candlesticks.

At Gran's one afternoon, Mum was upstairs packing her mother's clothes into bin bags ready to take to the charity shop while I was in the front room. I'd been given a couple of boxes to put Gran's candle collection in, which Mum wanted to keep as they'd been important to my granny. I was to put the candlesticks in one box and the candles in another.

Placing the boxes on the dining table, I went around

the room picking up a candlestick here and there, from brass three-armed candelabras to titchy black metal ones with a curved bit for your finger and glass tea light holders, the occasional tear rolling off the end of my nose.

At the back of the room was Granny Joy's bookcase with rows and rows of her romantic novels. There were also a few scented candles. Three years ago, my mum had helped me pick out a Christmas candle for my gran. I'd spotted one in a holder like a drinking glass that smelled of orange, cinnamon and cloves and had the word *Joy* on the side in gold writing, surrounded by gold stars.

'Rosie, this is my favourite scent *ever*!' Gran had said, delighted, when I'd handed it to her just before Christmas. After that, I bought her the same candle every year.

Granny Joy would burn them down, then wash out the glass they came in and keep them on her bookshelf. Here were the two empty ones, the new candle I'd given her the day before she died in the middle. The wax surface was smooth and pristine, the wick still white. I put it to my nose. The delicious spicy smell that reminded me of mince pies and Christmas cake and my gran was too much. That's when my tears really began to fall.

I sat on the sofa and sobbed and sobbed for my lovely, quirky, generous grandma, who'd always sneak a pound coin into my hand for crisps when Mum wasn't looking. She'd been an affectionate lady, often touching me on my shoulder or arm as she passed. Today, as I sat weeping and holding the *Joy* candle, I felt pressure on my shoulder, a squeezing. I knew it was her, and it was comforting, not scary.

But one thing that was very scary indeed were my dreams about the accident. Mum was wrong. They hadn't stopped after I'd seen Gran in the coffin. They'd got more frequent and become so terrifying I dreaded going to bed.

That night, the dream came. And it was bad.

It began in the usual way, with me coming to and realising I was outdoors, floating 10 feet above the ground by the bridge where Gran had died. It was part of a viaduct, and I knew the area as it was near our local cinema.

There on the ground lay my gran on her back,

face contorted with pain as she screamed. She'd worn an open-face helmet, which was still on her head. I couldn't hear anything, and I was grateful for that. But tonight, the scene was different.

The other five or so times, I'd been vaguely aware of a man with Gran. Tonight, I could clearly see he had pinched cheeks, a grey beard and wore a yellow and black woollen hat. He knelt by Gran, tying something around her leg, which stopped at the knee. The leather was ragged where her leg had been ripped off and there was so much blood. I wanted to look away but I couldn't. I had no choice but to stare at the terrible scene below me.

It was dark, early evening, and I could see frost sparkling on the pavement and damp patches on the man's white T-shirt between his shoulder blades, which I guess was sweat, even though the weather was freezing. My outer body felt nothing but emotionally, I felt sick and dizzy.

The man finished knotting what looked like a tartan scarf around the remains of gran's leg by the wound and took a phone from his back pocket. He spoke into it, very agitated, then threw it down, sat back and took

Granny Joy's hand. She was quieter now, moaning and rolling her head from side to side, agony written on every line of her face.

The scene was so shocking that, overwhelmed with sadness and fear, I managed to will myself to wake up. I fled crying into Mum and Dad's room and jumped on their bed.

'Mmm, lovie, another bad dream?' said Mum, half-opening her eyelids and seeing me there. 'Come on. Climb in.' She drew back the cover and, big girl that I was, I got in gratefully and let her put her arms around me. Dad hadn't stirred and Mum fell straight back to sleep.

As I lay in the dark with my back to my mum and her arms around my front, I felt a squeeze on my shoulder through the duvet. 'Oh, Granny,' I said, with a miserable sigh. 'Can you make these dreams stop? I can't stand them...'

In the morning after breakfast, Mum left to continue clearing Granny Joy's house. I couldn't bring myself to go again today. And I was a kid and wanted to see my friends, so I walked over to Leila's.

While I'd told my parents a bit about my

nightmares, Leila was the only person who knew the details. With both sets of grandparents alive, like normal people, Leila understood how hard I'd been hit by the loss of my gran.

'It's getting worse,' I told her, fiddling with the pony charm on my phone case. 'It's like I'm hovering above, watching. But last night, I could see every detail. But I don't know if it's real...'

'That's called an OOBE,' said Leila confidently. 'An out-of- the-body experience. When you're asleep, apparently a part of you – your etheric body – can float out of you and go on journeys and watch events. Did it happen on the night of the accident? Maybe your etheric body was there at the time.'

'My what now?' I asked.

'Your etheric body. You must have heard of people floating above their bodies during operations, seeing every detail, then telling the doctors what they saw when they wake up? I wish I could do that.'

'My first dream wasn't at the time Gran died – the accident was late in the afternoon,' I said, annoyed that my friend was making my awful experience about her. 'The dreams started the week after. And they are just dreams, anyway.'

Leila leaned forward. 'Are you certain the dreams didn't start until a while after the accident?'

'Of course.'

She tried another tack. 'Do you know exactly what happened at the accident and who was there?'

'I don't know the details, and neither does Mum. The inquest is coming up and we'll find out more then. Let's talk about something else.'

But I couldn't get Leila's words out of my head. An OOBE?

Walking the few blocks home, I pulled the collar of my padded coat tighter around my neck and stuck my gloved hands in my pockets. It had been raining and the fresh, green smell of the wet bushes I passed hung in the cold air, stinging my nostrils. I had my head down to keep an eye out for slippery patches on the icy pavement when suddenly the scent of the bushes was replaced by the aroma of orange, cinnamon and cloves. Granny Joy's candle! Yet it wasn't possible – was it?

I stopped to look over the fences of the houses nearest to me. Maybe someone was cooking a

Christmas dessert and the scent had floated out of one of the windows? But all the windows were shut. And it was so cold. Who would open a window on such a freezing day? Then I felt that touch on my shoulder, firm and definite. 'Thanks, Granny Joy,' I said out loud. 'It's tough without you and we miss you so much.'

Feeling foolish talking to myself in the middle of the street, I sped home.

In the kitchen later, I had an idea. 'Mum,' I said as she grilled sausages for tea, 'do you know exactly what happened at Granny Joy's accident? I know the police said the lorry driver whose wheels her bike went under sat with her while the ambulance came.'

'Can we not discuss this at teatime, Rosie?' she said, angrily stabbing holes in the sausages with a fork to stop them bursting. 'It's on my mind enough as it is. I don't know any details.'

But I was determined to find out more. 'Maybe you could ask for more info?'

'Why would I want to do that?' she snapped. 'The inquest is next year and I'll have to hear all about it then.'

Dad came in and I said no more while we ate.

I grabbed him later on the garden step while he was putting the bins out and asked whether he might be willing to find out what actually happened at the accident.

'I can't wait for the inquest, Dad,' I said, 'and anyway, I won't be going. I know the details will be horrible and upsetting but I need to know how much like my dream it was.'

We chatted a bit more and he understood my urgency. 'If it's that important to you, Rosie, I'll see what I can do.'

Five days later, I was in my room when the spicy cinnamon smell wafted under my nose. It hung around for a few minutes, then vanished. There was no touch on my shoulder this time, and I hadn't had the dream in several days, since the really nasty version I'd described to Leila. But I had a feeling it was due, and I shuddered.

Then came a tap on my door. It was Dad.

'Rosie, I have some news,' he said grimly. 'Let's sit on your bed.'

We perched on my Christmas quilt cover, with its

snowmen and sledges, and he took my hands in his.
'Your mum gave me permission to call the police,' he
said, 'and I spoke to one of the officers who attended
the scene of your gran's accident. I won't tell you
everything because it is very unpleasant, but what is
it you want to know?'

My stomach trembling with fear and anticipation, I
said, 'What did the man who helped Granny Joy look
like? The lorry driver? His clothes?'

'He had a grey beard and hair and wore a
lumberjack shirt and a woolly hat. The guy took his
shirt off to tie around your grandma's leg to stem the
bleeding. That's called making a tourniquet. It's what
you do if somebody's losing blood, if you can.'

'A lumberjack shirt?' I repeated. 'That's checked,
right?'

'Yes.'

'Then that's my dream, exactly.'

I described it to Dad, who shook his head. 'That's
not possible. You must have got mixed up somehow.
Maybe your mum did know, and you overheard her
telling somebody and both forgot?'

'No, that's not right, Dad,' I said firmly. 'I'd

remember.'

I went straight to Leila's and told her my discovery. 'I knew it!' she said. 'Astral projection. And OOBEs. I don't know how it worked in your case, but we all know you're weird in a good way. I always thought so.'

It was still a few days to Christmas. Back home, I took Granny Joy's new cinnamon candle from the boxes we'd stowed in the spare room, positioned it on the coffee table and lit it. As I breathed in the spicy scent, something told me I wouldn't have that terrible dream about her death again.

That was seven years ago, and I haven't had that or any other nightmares since, although I do sometimes catch that spicy aroma in the air.

Especially at Christmas time.

NEWSLETTER & FREE GIFT

Newsletter & Exclusive Gift

One of the best things about being an author is building a relationship with my readers. Your support allows me to keep writing my books and I appreciate that. So do join my monthly newsletter and keep in touch. There'll be subscriber-only content, true hauntings and fascinating facts, plus you'll be the first to hear about my new books. As a sign-up gift, you'll get an exclusive novella or true ghost story. Details on my website.

Visit **tinavantylerbooks.com** to sign up and tell me where to send your free gift. Bye for now!

To My Readers

I hope you enjoy this collection of spine-tinglers. If so, please consider leaving an honest review on Amazon to help fellow fear-fanciers who are considering buying this book. Thank you!

True Tales Of The Supernatural: Real Christmas Ghost Stories is the fifth in a series of real ghost story anthologies. Follow me on my Facebook page **@TinaVantylerBooks**, my TikTok **@SpookyTinaVT** or my Instagram **@tinavantylerauthor** for news and information about my stories and upcoming releases.

ALSO BY TINA VANTYLER

HAVE YOU READ THEM ALL?

Four more books in the Real Ghost Stories series:

TRUE TALES OF THE SUPERNATURAL FROM THE UK

12 brand-new accounts of real paranormal activity you won't find anywhere else, including: A stroll in the park that turned to terror in *On The One Hand;* an anniversary break that almost broke a husband and wife in *Floored;* a dream home that housed a fiend in *The Bad Man;* the horror that waited below in *Going Underground;* and a reminder to be careful what you wish for in *Not In My Back Yard.*

TRUE TALES OF THE SUPERNATURAL FROM THE UK VOLUME TWO

15 genuine heart-stopping encounters with phantoms and poltergeists, such as: The activity that terrified a paranormal investigator in *Bad Vibrations;* the former funeral parlour's foul visitor in *Up In Smoke;* the battle between feminine energy and masculine malevolence in *Someone To Watch Over Me;* the marrow-freezing expression of affection in *Different Strokes;* and the bloody pact that led to pandemonium in *Bonded By Blood.*

※

TRUE TALES OF THE SUPERNATURAL FROM THE UK & IRELAND VOLUME THREE

These 16 delightfully frightful, bone-chilling encounters with the undead will clasp you in a cold embrace and include: The mother so distraught that she couldn't tell right from wrong in *Death Becomes Her;* the terror wreaked by a jilted lover in *Full Throttle;* the merchant incensed by changes to his home in *Shop Of Horrors;* the nauseating stench that accompanied a ghastly guest in *Bedfellows;* and the disembodied head in the hallway in *Visitors*.

REAL GHOST STORIES: TRUE TALES OF HAUNTED TOYS VOLUME FOUR

15 original true tales of toys gone bad and innocence corrupted, such as: The ghastly gift from a damaged playmate in *The Doll;* the demonic fiend that pursued a family in *Memento Mori;* the diabolical package from a dead mother in *Ol' Blue Eyes Is Back;* the small visitor from beyond the grave in *David;* and the sinister mystery man in the photo in *In Pieces.*

One collection of short ghost fiction:

THE DOCTOR AT CUTTING CORNER AND OTHER GHOST STORIES: SPINE-TINGLING TALES OF THE SUPERNATURAL

Six ghost horror stories to torture your mind with

macabre images that will send icy shivers rippling down your spine, including: The surgeon with a bloody secret in *The Doctor At Cutting Corner;* the horror unleashed by accident in *Heads You Lose;* the vengeful fiend at a lonely train station on Christmas Eve in *Nipper;* and the gruesome act that lingered on in *The Ancestral Seat.*

ABOUT THE AUTHOR

The supernatural has fascinated journalist Tina Vantyler since she was a (weird!) child. The fact her mother kept her up late watching classic horror films and took Tina on outings to graveyards rather than playgrounds probably has something to do with her obsession.

Several supernatural experiences of her own, along with the terrifying testimonies of people Tina has spoken to, have confirmed for her that, as Mr Shakespeare said, 'There are more things in heaven and earth... than are dreamt of in your philosophy.'

Tina writes fiction and non-fiction about the paranormal.

Acknowledgments

A huge thank-you to those of you who shared your stories so generously. And many thanks to Lis and Oliver once again for their patience and support, and for casting their eye over the finished tales.

Printed in Great Britain
by Amazon

33763649R00099